# THE CYBORG'S RUNAWAY

## GALACTIC CLAN WARS
### BOOK TWO

SAMANTHA CHARLTON

*The Cyborg's Runaway*, by Samantha Charlton



Published by Winter Mist Press

ISBN: 978-1-99-117475-8 (paperback)

Edited by Tim Burton
Cover design by Winter Mist Press
Cover photography courtesy of www.despositphotos.com and www.pixabay.com

Visit Sam's website: www.samanthacharltonauthor.com

**He swore allegiance only to himself, until she gave him something worth fighting for.**

**Aria is a brilliant scientist. She's also engaged to a clan-lord.** It's a union she always knew would come, always accepted.

**But on her wedding day, she discovers a terrible secret. Horrified, Aria flees.**

**Vic used to be a space marine.** However, after he was badly wounded, and the transitioning to make him a cyborg went wrong, Vic went rogue. He's now part man, part machine—an outcast, a loner. These days, he works as a trader, and sometimes smuggler, on the hottest galactic routes.

**Vic's solitary existence comes to an end the day he saves Aria from those hunting her—an act that also makes him a wanted man.**

On the run together, runaway bride and cyborg soon form a powerful connection.

**Yet can it survive the tough decisions they must both face?**

*A runaway bride, the cyborg who rescues her, and an epic Space Opera Adventure. Book Two of The Galactic Clan Wars series, THE CYBORG'S RUNAWAY is a stand-alone romance in an exciting new space fantasy series.*

*"You can't run away from trouble.
There ain't no place that far."*
—Uncle Remus

**In another time …**
**In another galaxy …**

# 1. COLLISION

"YOU DRIVE A hard bargain, cyborg," the Vulkar growled. The hulking male had his hands on the table. Blunt fingers, tipped with sharp black talons, tapped the polished surface impatiently. "But I'm not giving those parts to you for less than five hundred hard credits."

Vic didn't break the Vulkar's stare. Leaning back in his seat, he let another silence draw out between them.

Fash wouldn't be able to read his face.

Vic didn't like the expressionless features that stared back at him when he looked in the mirror these days—but the blankness helped him at times when he met with clients. It made him look as if he had nerves of steel, as if warm blood didn't still pump through his veins.

Others found it unnerving. His blank face gave him the upper hand—and he liked that. It was just as well too, as irritation thrummed through him now. He knew Vulkars loved to haggle, but he couldn't be bothered these days.

"Four hundred," he drawled after a long pause. "It's a good deal, and you know it, Fash."

Fash Mir-Ferrin's heavy brow lowered over deep-set eyes, while his broad shoulders stiffened under his skin-tight tunic. Vic's gaze never wavered, although a slight flicker of concern did ignite in his gut.

Vulkars were notorious for their volcanic tempers and violent tendencies. Vic was a tall and well-built human cyborg male, but those huge hands could snap his neck like a twig.

Nonetheless, Vic had to move the stolen machinery parts on—he was taking a risk and needed to be paid well for it.

Fash knew how it worked.

Vulkar and cyborg sat in a dark, crowded bar. Pungent smoke from clove pipes hung low in the air. It was noisy enough in here to give the patrons privacy:

the jaunty strains of flutes two Crall were playing at one end blended with the rumble of voices.

Fash and Vic had taken a booth in the corner, a position that afforded them a view of the establishment while giving them the privacy their conversation required. Two empty glasses sat between them.

Vic fought the urge to drum his own fingers on the table. Damn it, these staring matches were wearing. He just wanted to agree on a price and get the merch loaded. Obsidian would be wondering where he'd gotten to. After they moved this shipment on, he and his first mate planned to take a much-needed vacation. They'd earned it.

"Four hundred and eighty," Fash muttered.

"Four hundred and twenty."

A low growl rumbled deep in the Vulkar's throat. His lips twisted, revealing a pair of sharp fangs.

Those teeth were another reason why you didn't want to piss off a Vulkar.

"All right then … four hundred and thirty," Vic said, careful to keep his voice as expressionless as his face. "But that's my last offer."

Muttering a curse, Fash withdrew a small, circular device from a pouch at his waist, a PCSD—a Portable Currency Storage Device containing hard credits—and slammed it down on the table between them. "Thief."

Vic didn't answer. Nonetheless, relief, and quiet satisfaction, glowed in his chest as he withdrew his own PCSD and connected it to the one before him. Although he'd started to feel jaded of late, Vic still enjoyed getting the upper hand in a deal. He tapped out the sum on the screen, and the device let out a low 'blip' as the transaction went through. "It's a pleasure doing business with you, Fash," he said, disconnecting the PCSD and slipping it back into a breast pocket on the utility vest he wore.

Fash grunted. "Where are you docked?"

"Landing Bay 60F."

"I'll contact one of my boys, and he'll bring a trolley around now."

Vic nodded and slid out of the booth. With the deal done, there was no point in him hanging around. He left the bar without another word, weaving his way through the tightly packed tables. A few curious glances followed him as he went. Vic ignored them—stares were something he was used to.

Cyborgs weren't usually found doing business in bars. They were drones, living in hives upon battleships. But Vic wasn't like his brethren. Six years earlier, he'd left that life behind him—and he was never going back.

Ever since his desertion, he'd established himself as a trader, and sometime smuggler, of machinery and weapons across the sector. However, a year earlier, he'd taken on a different sort of job—a dangerous mission, to rescue the Mir-Brennan clan-lord and his family. It had been high-risk, and he'd been paid well for it. But afterward, Vic had told himself that he'd stick to his usual line of work in the future. He preferred dealing in merch, not sector politics, or people.

Life was simpler that way.

Outside the bar, Vic stepped out onto a walkway and headed left. He needed to get back to the spaceport and collect the parts.

His heavy boots clanged on the metal plating, while his gaze swept over Lanthor's Rec Bubble. A cobweb of catwalks that led between bars, cafes, and restaurants filled the upper level of the sphere, while a large, rectangular park, lined by tall dark-blue trees, took up the ground floor. The resinous scent of the conifers wafted up, and Vic sucked in a lungful. After breathing in recycled air for weeks on end in space—and the cloying clove smoke inside the bar—he welcomed the sharp, sweet aroma of the conifers.

Lanthor was an asteroid space station—a huge, pitted rock studded with transparent spheres. It wasn't wealthy or beautiful, but it was a place you could find anything if you looked hard enough—and it was a regular stop for Vic. There were several individuals like Fash who moved stolen goods on from here.

Vic ascended the metal stairs to the next level and quickened his pace.

There was another reason he'd been eager to close the deal with the Vulkar. He already had a buyer for these hyperdrive parts, one who'd give him twice what he paid for them.

Fash didn't know that though. Best he never found out.

Halting on the transpod platform, Vic punched the call button on the panel next to a set of transparent doors. Clear tubes crisscrossed the asteroid, ferrying citizens and visitors via the transpod system from bubble to bubble.

He was waiting for the next pod, bound for the spaceport, deep in thought as he mentally charted the fastest route to Calberic—the planet where his client waited—when shouting roused him.

Hand going to the grip of the laser-pistol at his hip, he swiveled on his heel.

A human female raced toward him. The woman was striking, with dark-copper skin and a wild mane of chestnut hair cascading over her shoulders. The burgundy jumpsuit she wore molded to her tall, curvaceous form, while a deep-purple cloak flew out behind her.

She'd just shoved two Daksari out of the way, nearly sending the tall, slender 'water people' over the railings. However, the woman kept running. Her expression was resolute, her jaw set.

A second later, Vic spied two towering bronze figures at the end of the walkway she'd just fled along. They appeared to be chasing the woman, their rubber-soled feet pounding on metal as they steadily gained ground.

Vic's spine snapped straight.

*Mir-Ferrin battle-droids.*

Lanthor sat in the heart of Mir-Lelith territory. It was far from Platinum 5—the seat of the Mir-Ferrin clan—and not somewhere you'd expect to see Mir-Ferrin droids or soldiers.

The transpod arrived then, sliding to a halt with a hiss. The glass doors to the small, clear bubble opened, and a group of young human males wearing silver uniforms—Mir-Lelith marines on R&R—stumbled out, their drunken laughter echoing through the sphere.

The woman collided with them, struggling to get free as one of the men groped her.

Meanwhile, the battle-droids thundered closer.

Without thinking, Vic elbowed his way into the midst of the drunken marines, grabbed the woman by the arm, and hauled her into the transpod.

Slamming his palm onto the panel next to the doors, he drew his laser-pistol.

The doors needed to close—now. He'd engaged battle-droids before and had fought *alongside* them many times. The armor they wore was difficult to put a scratch on. Their weak spot was the back of the head, where their metal skulls met the neck, but if he started shooting, he risked hitting one of the drunken marines.

The men in question had just seen the advancing battle-droids, and they lurched out of the way to let them pass.

The doors slid shut, just as the droids closed in, their red eyes burning into Vic.

An instant later, the doors sealed, and the transpod sped off, leaving the woman's pursuers pounding metal fists uselessly against the tempered glass.

Turning, Vic shifted his attention to his companion.

She was leaning against the wall, her full breasts rising and falling in sharp, rapid movements as she stared through the glass at the battle-droids she'd just escaped.

"You're safe," Vic announced after a pause. "For the moment at least. There's a pod to the spaceport every ten minutes … so you're going to have to move fast."

The woman shifted her attention to him—and her large dark-green eyes widened just a fraction when she saw who, or what, her savior was.

Vic tensed. He should be used to women's reactions to him by now, but it still cut him. They didn't see a human male when they looked at him, they saw a cyborg: half man, half machine. The black plate that covered his right eye dominated his face.

"It's all right," he said, his tone cooling. "I'm not as dangerous as I look."

Their gazes locked, and then, to his surprise, her full lips stretched into a genuine smile—an expression that made him catch his breath.

"Thank you." Her voice was low, husky—sensual. "I really appreciate your quick thinking back there."

"You're welcome," he replied gruffly, taken aback by her response.

The woman's gaze never left his face. "You're a cyborg?"

"Yeah … a rogue one." He inclined his head then. "What do Mir-Ferrin battle-droids want with you?"

The woman raised a hand and pushed a heavy lock of chestnut hair off her face. She then grimaced. "It's complicated." She glanced back over her shoulder at the receding Rec Bubble, as if to check the battle-droids weren't clawing their way down the tunnel toward her. "Did you say we were heading to the spaceport?"

"Yes."

"Good." She heaved a loud sigh and adjusted the backpack she wore under her cloak. "I need to get out of here."

Vic observed her profile, curiosity spiraling up within him. She had fine, aristocratic bone structure, and her accent was high-born. She might not want to tell him why the Mir-Ferrins were chasing her, but she unwittingly gave much about herself away.

He caught himself then. *Stay out of it, Mir-Riorde. Who cares who she is or why she's running?*

# 2. WE'RE LEAVING

BRACING HERSELF AGAINST the railing that ran around the circular transpod, Aria Mir-Straken concentrated on taking slow, deep breaths to try and calm the rapid beat of her heart.

*How did they find me here?*

She'd fled Haliaen over a week earlier, aboard a passenger liner bound for Mir-Lelith territory—and she'd been hopping from place to place ever since.

But, somehow, her fiancé's henchmen were always just one step behind her.

And this time, they'd caught up with her.

If the cyborg hadn't acted quickly, and dragged her into the safety of the transpod, they'd have captured her.

*The cyborg.*

Aria's attention flicked back to the tall, broad-shouldered figure standing near the pod doors. Dressed in dark-grey cargo pants and a utility vest, and wearing heavy black boots, he carried himself with the ramrod posture of a trained soldier.

She'd glimpsed a few cyborgs over the years—for they patrolled Platinum 5, where she'd visited regularly as a child and teenager.

Apart from his clothing—for the ones she'd seen wore armor—this man looked just like the cyborgs she remembered. Instead of his right eye, he bore a grim black plate. But it was his facial expression that gave him away. Blank—as if no thoughts moved through his mind, as if no feelings troubled him.

Most people found cyborgs unnerving, many even feared them. But Aria didn't share the aversion. Whenever she'd seen cyborgs in the past, she'd felt empathy for them. Once they'd been men, space marines who'd fallen in service to their clan-lords.

The Gods had dealt them a cruel fate indeed.

And yet the cyborg standing a few feet away was different. He'd saved her. And the man's face might have been expressionless, but his good eye and his voice weren't. In just a few words, he'd revealed a dry sense of humor and sharp intelligence.

Aria was focused on escaping the battle-droids—on getting off Lanthor before they caught up with her again—but she was intrigued by her savior, nonetheless. What was his story?

"We're here," the cyborg announced, glancing her way as the transpod slid to a stop. "I'd disappear if I were you."

Aria nodded. "I intend to."

Her pulse, which had steadied during the transpod journey, sped up once more.

She had to keep running.

After what she'd discovered back on Haliaen, after the conversation she'd overheard, she couldn't let Elijah catch up with her.

Aria pushed herself off the railing, pulled up her hood, and approached the doors, before glancing once more at the cyborg. "Thanks again." She flashed her savior another smile. However, this one was brittle as nerves clutched at her stomach.

The doors whispered open, revealing a crowd of impatient travelers. The cyborg exited in front of Aria, and the crowd parted for him. One or two of the travelers cast him nervous looks, but he strode on. He entered the terminal ahead of her before turning right, in the direction of the private landing bays.

Aria turned left and hurried into the terminal. Like the other habitable zones on Lanthor, the spaceport was a vast, clear bubble. However, this one was lined with docking stations, where several craft waited.

Glancing over her shoulder, on the lookout for bronze armored figures bearing down on her, Aria quickened her pace.

She took the cyborg's advice then, not wasting any time.

Heading across the floor, she intercepted a ticketing-droid. The small silver droid floated through the crowd, amber lights flickering on its domed head.

"When's the next departure?" she asked.

"There's a passenger liner for Marcil II, in the Belar System, in twenty minutes," the droid chirped back.

Aria sucked in a deep breath. "That's perfect … I'll take a one-way ticket."

Marcil II was a large, heavily populated planet where she could hopefully disappear for good. It was also in the midst of Mir-Brennan territory. Mir-Ferrin battle-droids might hesitate to follow her there, for those two clans were enemies now. The Mir-Brennans wouldn't welcome Mir-Ferrin ships in their systems.

In fact, she was lucky to find a ship that would take her into Mir-Brennan territory. Up until recently, the Mir-Brennans and the Mir-Leliths had been locked in conflict—which meant they'd cut commercial flights between the territories. But of late, the two clans had negotiated an official ceasefire, and flights had resumed.

Aria fumbled for the PCSD in her bag and paid for the ticket, pushing the device against a screen on the front of the ticketing-droid. The device beeped at her before showing the remaining balance.

Aria's brow furrowed. She still had funds, but they were starting to dwindle. She couldn't keep running forever, but neither could she return to Haliaen. Her father would be furious with her for running out on her fiancé. He wouldn't understand her reasons, or likely even believe them. Amongst the ruling families of the galactic clans, duty and loyalty to one's own was everything.

Her pulse accelerated further. Surely, Elijah would give up eventually. Perhaps he'd find someone else to do his bidding. Although, if he ever discovered she knew about the biological weapon they were developing, he'd put a price on her head.

Heat ignited under Aria's ribcage then—not for the first time since she'd fled her home planet—fury enveloping her.

How dare the Mir-Ferrins flout the Gods like this.

They were playing with fire.

She'd spent the last decade researching viruses and bacteria that affected sentient beings, how they mutated and replicated. Science was powerful, and it had to be respected.

She couldn't believe Elijah had agreed to his brother's twisted plan—but she refused to be part of it.

The ticketing-droid spat out a small, transparent ticket. "Gate 14," it informed her. "Boarding has commenced … please go straight to the gate."

Aria nodded, taking the ticket, and stepping away from the droid.

Raised voices behind her intruded then.

Her gaze traveled to where two battle-droids cut a swathe through the throng—shoving travelers out of the way—straight toward her.

Panic grasped Aria by the throat, squeezing tight.

"Damn it," she muttered, glancing around and frantically searching for Gate 14.

However, when she saw the slow-moving line of passengers in front of it, her heart started kicking against her ribs.

She wouldn't escape in that direction.

There was no time to think, no time to come up with a plan. Instead, she dove right through the crowd.

Shouting rang across the terminal behind her.

She knew, without needing to glance over her shoulder, that the droids had given chase and were plowing their way through the press of travelers to reach her. She imagined them trampling anyone in their path. The battle-droids were relentless; they didn't need to sleep, eat, or rest.

No matter where she went, they followed.

For the first time since she'd run from Haliaen, despair clutched at Aria's throat. *It's pointless to keep running—they'll catch me in the end.* But even as part of her knew it was futile, she increased her pace, using her elbows to cleave a path through the crowd. Her hood fell back, but she didn't care.

There had to be another way out of this terminal.

She wasn't giving up just yet.


Vic watched the Vulkar roll the empty trolley down the ramp, out of the hold of his freighter. From the back, *The Wayfarer* appeared brand-new these days. However, it wasn't. The rear of his ship had been rebuilt a year earlier—after sustaining serious damage during a mission.

Vic had paid close attention while Fash's associate had unloaded the drives, to ensure he was getting what he'd paid for.

You could never be too careful in his line of work, but although Fash was a criminal, he knew better than to double-cross one of his best clients.

"It's a pleasure doing business with you," he said as the Vulkar dragged the trolley toward the landing bay doors. "As always."

He received a grunt in reply.

Shaking his head—Fash's crew were a surly lot—Vic moved to the side of the hull, slamming the heel of his hand on a narrow panel.

With a hiss, the cargo hold ramp closed.

Meanwhile, the Vulkar exited the landing bay, entered the brightly lit corridor beyond, and turned left.

Vic was about to look away when a flash of burgundy and flying chestnut hair caught his eye.

The woman he'd helped earlier sprinted past, glancing his way as she did so.

Vic stilled. What was she doing at this end of the spaceport?

Seconds later, the woman appeared once more, barreling toward him.

"What are—" he began, but she cut him off.

"Sorry about this," she gasped. "But I need somewhere to hide!"

To his surprise, the woman veered left, away from where he stood behind the hull of *The Wayfarer,* and fled up the passenger ramp into the belly of the freighter.

"Shit." Vic started moving toward where she'd just disappeared when a rasping metallic voice echoed across the landing bay.

"Halt!"

His gaze cut to the entrance to see two battle-droids bearing down on him, laser-rifles raised.

Vic drew the pistol at his hip and dove for the ramp, just as they fired on him.

Laser bolts ricocheted off *The Wayfarer's* thick Lazda steel shields, narrowly missing Vic. He dropped, rolled, and made it to the hatch, returning fire on the droids. Slipping into the entranceway, he slammed his hand down on the button next to the hatch, and the ramp lifted with a hiss of hydraulics, sealing him inside.

The freighter shuddered as rounds of laser hit it.

Cursing loudly, Vic stormed forward, up the narrow passageway.

He found the woman plastered against the far wall of the cabin, her green eyes wide with fright.

A lanky battle-droid, this one clad in black armor rather than bronze, faced her, a laser-pistol trained on the woman's chest. Twin crimson eyes fixed her with an unblinking stare.

"You've met Obsidian, I see," Vic greeted her.

The woman's throat bobbed. "Is it going to shoot me?"

"Not unless I ask him to." Vic moved past his first mate toward the cockpit. The freighter's fuselage creaked ominously. "Put the gun away, Obsidian ... we're leaving."

# 3. THE RUNAWAY BRIDE

"STRAP YOURSELF IN," the cyborg ordered, falling into the chair next to his droid copilot. "This could get rough."

Pulse jumping in her throat, Aria pushed herself off the wall and staggered across to the row of seats behind the cockpit. She collapsed into the first one and fumbled with the harness.

Meanwhile, the freighter rocked and shuddered as her pursuers continued firing on it.

"Your friends don't give up easily, do they?" her savior muttered. His hands flew over the controls, and the ship's engines pulsed into life, the deck beneath Aria's feet vibrating.

She didn't answer.

No, the battle-droids her fiancé had sent after her wouldn't give up—ever.

Despair twisted her belly as she imagined them tearing open the ramp to this ship and storming inside.

There was no way the cyborg and his droid copilot could protect her then.

And why should they? She was a stranger to them.

She shouldn't have run onto this ship without a care—but she'd been desperate. And she still was.

The engine pitch increased to a whine, and then the ship was turning, its arrow-like nose angling toward the open hangar doors. Space yawned before them.

A loud, insistent bleeping began then in the cockpit, and the sound didn't let up. "What's that?" Aria called out. Her nerves were stretched to breaking point as it was, and that noise didn't bode well.

"Tower Control," the cyborg replied curtly. "Our take-off slot isn't for another hour. They'll be wondering why I've started the engines."

Aria swallowed hard. "Can they stop us from leaving?"

"No, but I'll get fined."

The freighter rocked sideways, a loud 'boom' echoing through the landing bay.

"Great," the cyborg snarled. "They're lobbing detonators at us now."

"The shields are all raised," the droid rasped. It loomed over its companion, barely fitting into the copilot's chair. Aria watched, with rapt fascination, the battle-droid's clawed hands working the controls. When she'd set eyes on Obsidian, her heart had nearly stopped. She was still having difficulty accepting that these two were a team.

"Detonators?" Aria's mouth went dry.

"That's right," the captain muttered. "They'd better not damage my ship. I've only just had it repaired." He cut a look to his copilot. "Ready?"

"Yes, Vic."

The cyborg glanced over his shoulder, his single hazel eye spearing Aria. "Strapped in?"

"Yes."

"Here we go then." He slowly pulled back on a lever, and the freighter lifted off its landing pad. An instant later, he shoved the handle forward, and the ship roared out of the landing bay and into the void of space beyond.

The abruptness of their take-off threw Aria back in her seat, leaving her stomach far behind her.

The bleeping in the cockpit seemed to grow even louder then, hysterical almost, until it cut off.

Aria let out a sharp exhale. She closed her eyes, allowing the adrenaline that coursed through her veins to ebb a little.

*I escaped.*

She had, although only barely. And without the cyborg, who'd come to her aid twice, the battle-droids would have her now.

Sinking into her seat, her limbs suddenly weak, she let herself recover. However, when the engine noise changed pitch, and an invisible hand pressed her back in her seat, she opened her eyes to see they'd made the jump into hyperspace: the lights outside the cockpit window were now distorted streaks.

Unclipping herself, Aria got unsteadily to her feet. "You're making a habit of saving me," she said, forcing a lightness into her voice she didn't feel. "Thank you, once again."

The cyborg swiveled around in his chair, his gaze focusing on her once more. His impassive expression frustrated her. She was used to being able to read people well. "You hardly gave me a choice this time, did you?"

Aria huffed a nervous laugh. "No, I suppose not." Her belly tightened then. She hoped he wasn't angry. He certainly didn't seem happy to have her onboard his ship. She flashed the cyborg a smile then, hoping to thaw his grumpy mood. "I'm sorry your ship got fired on … and for the fine. I hope it's not too high."

"So do I," he drawled.

"I can pay it, if you like?"

"That would be appreciated."

Aria's smile faltered. He hadn't missed a beat before accepting.

The cyborg got to his feet and stepped down into the cabin. "You shouldn't make empty offers."

"I wasn't," she replied, affronted. They now stood a couple of feet apart. She was a tall woman and didn't need to raise her gaze far to meet his.

"But you thought I'd do the noble thing and refuse, didn't you?"

Aria cocked an eyebrow before digging into her backpack for her PCSD. "How much do I owe you?"

His gaze glinted. "I won't hear from the Lanthor authorities until we come out of hyperspace, but five hundred credits should cover it."

Aria sucked in a sharp breath. That was steep, especially with her balance ever-dwindling. But she could hardly argue it, not when he'd whisked her away from Lanthor and transported her to safety.

Choking back a complaint, she nodded.

Wordlessly, the cyborg retrieved his own PCSD from the pocket of the grey utility vest he wore and passed it to her.

"Five hundred it is," she agreed, connecting their devices, and punching out the sum on hers. Her PCSD flashed orange and emitted a low bleep, letting her know the transaction had gone through. She handed him back his device before pocketing her own. "I'm happy to pay your fine, you know?" she murmured. "It's the least I can do after you saved me."

The cyborg scratched his clean-shaven jaw, his single hazel eye studying her. "About that ..."

Aria tensed. Of course, he'd be curious. Who wouldn't be? She stepped forward and thrust out her right hand. "First things first ... I'm Aria Mir-Straken."

He hesitated before taking her hand and shaking it. "And I'm Vic Mir-Riorde ... you've already been introduced to my first mate, Obsidian."

"I have."

Vic's grip was warm and strong, and Aria found herself wanting to hold on. Pushing aside the odd desire, she dropped her hand to her side and tried to ignore the strange tingling in her palm.

The cyborg's attention never wavered from her face. "Are you going to tell me why those battle-droids were hunting you?"

Aria sighed. "As I said in the transpod ... it's complicated."

"I've got time."

His laconic tone made her mouth curve once more. She reached up, massaging a tense muscle in her shoulder. "I don't suppose you've got something to drink?"

"The water dispenser is behind you."

"Something stronger ... a glass of wine maybe?"

His mouth twitched. It was the closest he came to showing any facial expression, almost as if he was trying to smile. "I've got some Morith Whisky ... will that do?"

Aria hesitated. In truth, she wasn't much of a spirits drinker. However, her nerves were fried right now. She needed to unwind. "Yes, thanks."

Aria moved to the small table at the back of the cabin, sliding onto the bench seat, and rested her elbows on its smooth surface. She watched Vic reach into a cabinet and produce a tall bottle of amber-hued liquid and two cut-glass tumblers.

"I'll join you." He then glanced her way. "Ice?"

Aria nodded.

He shoved one of the tumblers into the water dispenser and pressed a button: ice cubes rattled into it. Pouring them two fingers of whisky each—Aria noted he took his whisky neat—Vic carried them across to the table. He slid Aria's glass across to her before taking a seat opposite.

Picking up her drink, she took a large, grateful sip before stifling a grimace. No, she'd never been a fan of hard liquor. Nonetheless, it had the desired effect; fire burned down her throat, igniting in her belly, and steadying her hands.

For the first time since the battle-droids had caught up with her today, the tension deep in her chest unraveled.

Aria heaved a deep sigh. "That's better." She took another sip before raising her gaze to Vic's face. He was handsome, in a rugged way. His ugly metal eye plant had drawn her attention initially, but it didn't now.

"I was to be married," she began after a long pause. "To Elijah Mir-Ferrin."

Vic leaned back slightly, his fingers tightening around his glass. "The Mir-Ferrin clan-lord?"

"Yes."

"*Was?*"

Aria cleared her throat. "I ran away on our wedding day ... and his battle-droids are hunting me."

Silence fell while Vic digested her words. He took a sip of whisky before swirling his glass. "Was it an arranged marriage?"

"It was … but I was happy enough to go through with it." Aria paused then, wondering at her own passivity. Truthfully, her research was her world; she'd never been interested in marriage. Her union with Elijah, whom she'd always liked, had made sense—plus it kept her father happy. "My father's the Mir-Straken clan-lord," she continued, feeling the need to explain herself. "Elijah and I were promised to each other very young. However, we've always been friends."

Vic inclined his head. "So, why run?"

Aria dragged in a deep breath and lifted her glass to her lips, taking another sip. She needed to fortify herself to tell the rest. "On the morning of our wedding, I overheard Elijah talking to his brother," she said, her voice lowering. "I discovered they're developing a biological weapon … a super-bacterium they plan to unleash upon the Mir-Brennans … and they want me to help them."

Her pulse sped up then. Just saying the words out loud was a reminder of why she'd run—and why she'd keep running.

A nerve on Vic's cheek flickered, his good eye narrowing. "A super-bacterium?"

"It's called Starellusbacter … and it kills fast."

"And where do you come in?"

"I'm a virologist, one of the best in the sector." The comment was said without boasting or vanity; it was a mere fact. She'd worked hard to build her reputation. "They need to control the thing they've created … to find a cure for it in case it ever spread to Mir-Ferrin planets or stations. That's what they need me for." Aria paused, her stomach clenching. "Elijah agreed to lie to me to get my assistance." Her voice caught then. "But I'm not marrying anyone who'd consider developing or unleashing such a weapon."

Vic nodded. "Is that why your fiancé wants you back then?"

Aria shook her head. "Elijah doesn't know I overheard him." She paused there, raking a hand through her hair.

To her consternation, her hand shook slightly. "And it's best he never finds out."

Aria watched as Vic drained the last of his whisky and set the glass down carefully in front of him. His gaze had shuttered, as if he was deep in thought.

Silence fell then, drawing out before Aria sighed. "Perhaps I should warn the Mir-Brennans."

Vic met her eye once more. "You probably should." He paused then before huffing a deep breath. "How about I take you to Staturine II?"

Aria leaned forward. Her pulse, which had just started to steady, took off again. She couldn't believe he was making such a generous offer. "Really?"

Vic nodded. "However, I've already set a course for Calberic, so we'll head there first. I've got a delivery to make … one that can't wait."

# 4. EXCEPTIONS

VIC POURED THEM each another whisky as he considered Aria Mir-Straken's story. It was an outlandish one, yet there was no lie in her emerald eyes. The woman had an expressive, honest face. He marked the disgust that shadowed her gaze when she spoke about the Starellusbacter—the 'super-bacterium'.

She was likely telling the truth.

And if she was—the tale was an alarming one.

Of course, Jenna Mir-Brennan had to be told. Despite Vic's nomadic existence—and that he answered to no one but himself these days—the Mir-Brennan clan-lady had earned his respect.

Jenna had hired Vic to help rescue her family from Idral around a year earlier. That rescue mission had been partially successful. Jenna's brother, the Mir-Brennan clan-lord, had died, but at least they'd managed to get his wife and daughter out. Afterward, Jenna became the clan leader, and she'd offered Vic the role of Captain of the Lady's Watch, the head of her personal bodyguard. Vic had been flattered by her trust in him, yet he'd refused.

That rescue mission had been a paid job—Jenna knew that.

His freedom was too valuable to give up, even for her. He didn't have time for most people, but he had a good opinion of Jenna Mir-Brennan and her consort, Malik.

Sliding back onto the bench seat opposite Aria, he passed her a fresh tumbler. Vic could tell she hadn't enjoyed the drink that much. Nonetheless, she was still on edge after her narrow escape. If anyone needed a drink right now, this woman did.

"I don't like the sound of that bio-weapon," he admitted eventually. "I don't blame you for running."

Across the table, Aria's full mouth tightened. "I can't believe Elijah is going to all this trouble to get me back."

Vic shrugged, even as he tried not to stare at her lips. He wasn't surprised the clan-lord wanted to retrieve his fiancée. The woman was gorgeous—with her copper skin, russet hair, long limbs, and dangerous curves.

Cyborgs weren't supposed to have sexual urges, but then Vic wasn't like the others. His brethren were impotent and infertile. They had just one purpose—to fight. However, a couple of days after he'd awoken from his failed 'transitioning', Vic had discovered that his manhood still functioned in the way it always had. He still had a sex drive but had no idea whether he'd ever be able to father children.

Infertility didn't bother him though; it was for the best.

Vic still noticed women, although they no longer wanted to have anything to do with him. After deserting Mir-Ferrin space fleet, he'd had to make do by servicing himself in the shower and paying the odd visit to pleasure houses.

"Some men don't like being made fools of," he murmured, tearing his gaze from those soft, sensual lips. "However, if he was relying on you helping to find a cure for this bacterium, then that might also explain his desperation."

Aria sighed. "I just hope those battle-droids don't follow us ... I can't seem to shake them."

"You can relax," he assured her. "*The Wayfarer* is fast ... they'll never catch us."

Aria's lips curved, and as when she'd flashed him that smile in the transpod, the expression made Vic's breathing still. "So, you're a trader?"

He nodded. "Most of the time."

His response was cagey, deliberately so. The truth was that Vic didn't like to go into detail about his line of work.

Aria cleared her throat then, her expression cautious. "So, how does a cyborg come to live independently from the hive?"

Vic took a long, slow sip of whisky. If he didn't like talking about his job much, he enjoyed talking about being a cyborg even less. Nonetheless, some subjects were difficult to avoid. "Until six years ago, I was a marine in the Mir-Ferrin space fleet," he said finally. "I took a laser bolt to the chest during a skirmish with pirates and was brought in for 'transitioning'."

Aria held his eye. She'd recovered now, after telling him about why she was running, and her gaze was direct, level. There was no trace of pity on her face, which he was grateful for—just empathy, and curiosity. She was a scientist, after all, he supposed.

Reaching up, Vic tapped the eye plant embedded into his right eye socket. He then rapped his knuckles against a hard plate on the right side of his chest. "Half man, half machine ... but something went wrong. When I woke up, it didn't take me long to realize that although I was stronger and faster than before ... I was still 'me'."

Aria took a gulp of whisky, her gaze widening. "That must have been terrifying," she whispered.

"It was."

"You told no one, I gather?"

He shook his head. "They'd just send me back into surgery to do the job properly." Inhaling slowly, Vic pushed down memories of the queasy horror that had stolen over him when he'd reached up and touched the metal plate over his right eye for the first time. "I played the game at first ... pretended to be just like the others." He paused then. "I lasted a couple of weeks ... and when I deserted, I took one of their battle-droids with me."

Aria glanced toward the cockpit, her features tightening. "You mean ... it once served the Mir-Ferrin clan-lord?"

"He did ... but I had Obsidian reprogrammed and replaced his armor. Bronze is too distinctive."

She favored him with an arch look. "The battle-droid obeys you now?"

"Obsidian *follows* me," he corrected her. "Like me, he has free will."

Aria stared back at him. And despite that she was trying to hide it, he marked the disbelief in her eyes. "Droids don't have free will," she said after a pause.

"Neither do cyborgs, apparently," he replied, holding his glass up to her in a mocking toast. "But I'm proof there are exceptions."

Aria climbed up onto the top bunk and sprawled out.

Two whiskies on an empty stomach had done the trick. Her body now felt languid and loose. The battle-droids and her treacherous fiancé no longer loomed large in her mind.

Lying on her back, Aria stared up at the dull-grey panels above her. Her limbs sank into the mattress. They still had a few hours before Calberic; she should get some sleep.

However, despite that the whisky had relaxed her, she was wide awake.

Inclining her head left, she surveyed the cabin of *The Wayfarer*. The freighter was utilitarian: functional grey, without adornment of any kind. The air in here was cooler than she was used to, and she shivered, pulling a blanket over her.

Vic moved past then, exiting the cabin, and walking out into the narrow passageway beyond, the doors whispering shut behind him.

His arms were bare, yet he didn't seem to notice the chill. He was a cyborg, after all—and they were programmed to deal well with fluctuations in temperature.

Aria's gaze lingered upon the doors he'd disappeared through, and she mulled over the cyborg's story.

There was no doubt about it: Vic Mir-Riorde was an enigma. A contradiction.

He'd helped her without hesitation, and yet their earlier conversation had revealed that he was a pragmatic loner with a cynical edge.

She could hardly blame him though.

The man had been dealt a rough deal.

Sighing, Aria turned her attention back to the ceiling. She closed her eyes, and exhaustion barreled into her. The hum and throb of the engines, as the freighter sped through hyperspace toward its destination, had a lulling effect.

The last week, since she'd fled Haliaen, had passed by in a blur of spaceports. After overhearing her betrothed and his brother in the gardens on her wedding morning, she'd returned to her apartment and moved fast. She'd not even bothered to pack a travel bag, for if any of the staff or guests saw her hurrying away from her father's manor house with luggage, they'd have alerted her father.

Instead, she selected a small backpack and filled it with essentials: a PCSD, a couple of nutri-bars, a canister of water, a few changes of underwear, deodorant, and her tablet.

The last thing she'd done before slipping out of her apartment was to disable the geo-locators on her tablet and wrist-comm.

She didn't want her fiancé, or her father, using them to track her down.

Donning a hooded cloak, she'd left the clan-lord's residence and made her way into town. The spaceport was busy, as always, and she'd taken the first passenger-liner off the planet.

She'd been running, and constantly looking over her shoulder, ever since.

Even on passenger liners, she'd been nervous, careful to keep to herself, with one watchful eye on the other passengers. There were space marshals on most scheduled flights; no doubt they'd been alerted that the Mir-Straken clan-lord's daughter was missing.

But now, thanks to Vic, she was safe. After a brief stop on Calberic, they'd be heading into Mir-Brennan territory—and owing to the hostilities between that clan and the Mir-Ferrins, it was unlikely her fiancé's battle-droids would follow her to Staturine II.

At last, she could lower her defenses.

The whisky and exhaustion dragged her down, and finally, Aria fell asleep.

# 5. A WHISPERING CONSCIENCE

ARIA GAZED UPON the small planet they now approached. She stood in the cockpit, behind Vic and Obsidian. They'd just come out of hyperspace, and the pilots were guiding *The Wayfarer* into Calberic's atmosphere.

Its swirling white, blue, and grey surface was beautiful, as were most planets from above. However, the entire planet was covered in ice.

Thousands of years earlier, Calberic had been a temperate planet, but then it had changed tilt and orbit, and an ice age had begun. The polar caps had slowly crept toward the equator, covering once verdant farmland with snow. The forests had died, and plant and animal life had become extinct.

But despite this decline, one that had made the planet largely uninhabitable for most life forms, Calberic had somehow thrived.

Its populace had built high, fully self-sufficient cities, and set the planet up as a center of commerce.

"Take a seat, Aria," Vic said then, putting on a headset. "We're about to make our approach."

She moved back into the cabin and did as bid, strapping herself in.

Moments later, the freighter's fuselage started to shudder.

"Tower, this is *The Wayfarer*." Vic's voice filtered out of the cockpit. "Permission requested to land at Fort Elisik."

A pause followed while Tower Control replied.

"I'm delivering machinery parts," he said after a few beats. "Copy … I'm sending you my trade permit now."

Aria gnawed at her bottom lip. She hoped Tower Control didn't ask too many questions—like if *The Wayfarer* was carrying any passengers.

However, moments passed, and they didn't.

A short while later, they were flying over a spine of glistening-white mountains toward Calberic's southern capital.

From a distance, Fort Elisik appeared like another mountain: a massive bulk rising from a snow-covered plain. But as they sped closer, Aria spied twinkling lights upon its surface, and when they drew closer still, the city itself became visible.

The surface of the great fortress bristled with landing bays, antennae, lights, and gleaming windows. A transparent tube—a transpod tunnel—curled its way up the exterior like a varicose vein. Snow swirled around Fort Elisik, obscuring the rising sun behind it.

"Landing Bay 441X," Vic instructed Obsidian.

The freighter dipped, angling toward the base of the city, and as they drew closer still, flashing orange lights beckoned them to their destination.

A hangar door was opening, and *The Wayfarer* slid into the bay, coming to a rumbling halt upon the landing pad.

Vic cut the engines and whipped off his headset before swiveling in his seat to face his passenger. "I shouldn't be long." There was an edge to his voice—guilt perhaps, she wondered. The Mir-Ferrins were developing a bioweapon that could destroy them all, and here he was focusing on earning some credits.

Unclipping her harness and rising to her feet, Aria shouldered her backpack. "I'm disembarking too," she informed him. "I need to do some shopping."

His hazel eye narrowed. "Shopping? Is this the time for that?"

Ignoring his terse tone, Aria shrugged. They really had to get to Staturine II, but since they'd made this detour, she would make use of it. "You might have noticed that I travel light." She arched an eyebrow then.

"And if you must know ... I've run out of clean underwear."

Vic muttered something under his breath, yet Aria ignored his protest. "Don't worry, I don't intend to linger on this ice-cube any longer than necessary. We need to see Jenna Mir-Brennan, remember?" She moved past him, toward the passageway. "I'm heading to the nearest mall to buy what I need ... and I'll meet you back here."

Descending the ramp into the landing bay, Aria glanced around, her body automatically tensing. Force of habit. Everywhere she looked these days, she expected to see battle-droids.

However, she needed to remind herself that they wouldn't find her here.

The bay was busy. *The Wayfarer* sat at the end of a line of freighters and small private passenger vessels. Ground staff moved around the ships, plugging in fuel lines, unloading baggage and cargo, and attaching hoses to effluent tanks.

Aria moved to the rim of the landing pad and glanced back at the freighter behind her. On Lanthor, she'd been too panicked to take a good look at the ship. She recognized the arrowhead shape: all the Mir-Ferrin vessels, from the humble freighters to fighters and immense battle cruisers, had the same distinctive, sleek lines.

Aria's mouth curved. She wouldn't be surprised if Vic had stolen this ship when he deserted. She wondered at the adventures he'd had since then—of the things he'd seen and done over the past few years.

What would it be like to live like that—traveling the sector, living from one job to the next? Vic's life made her own career choice seem safe and boring.

Turning away from the freighter, she descended the ramp from the landing pad. Heading toward the landing bay exit, she caught sight of the engraved emblem of a silver full moon with a shooting star above it upon the doors. Of course, Calberic was one of the jewels in the

Mir-Lelith crown. The clan motto, 'We do not forget' was emblazoned in embossed letters beneath the crest.

Aria's mouth curved into a rueful smile. The three ruling clans all had stark, aggressive mottos. She preferred her clan's own. The Mir-Strakens were 'Brighter than the Stars'. She'd always found those words inspiring, a reminder that the Mir-Strakens were innovators, researchers, and scientists. Their peaceful planet, Haliaen, was an incubator for some of the galaxy's greatest discoveries.

The landing bay doors opened with a whoosh, and she walked through them, quickening her step.

Standing before his ship, Vic watched Aria disappear.

He hoped she would make her shopping trip as brief as possible. Although this detour was his idea, he wouldn't be impressed if he returned to *The Wayfarer* and she was missing. The last thing he needed was to go hunting for her. Fort Elisik was huge.

Irritation spiked through him then. He hadn't known the woman long, yet already she was becoming a worry he didn't need.

"This is why I don't take passengers," he muttered to himself. "Too much fucking trouble."

Turning, he spied Obsidian descending the ramp. The droid's blood-red gaze settled upon him, expectant. It was the reminder Vic needed that he had business to conduct here. Once that was done, they could focus on getting to Staturine II.

*This should really wait until you've spoken to Jenna.*

Vic ignored his whispering conscience. Time was money, and it was vital he off-loaded the hyperdrives today. He couldn't miss out on this deal.

"When are you meeting the client?" Obsidian asked, his metallic voice carrying over the landing pad.

Vic glanced down at his wrist-comm, adjusting it to local time. "I told Crux I'd contact him once we'd docked," he replied. "I'll set up a rendezvous now."

"Do you want me to come with you?"

Vic looked up, considering the offer. Back on Lanthor, he'd met with Fash alone, but the Vulkar, although intimidating to look at, wasn't like Crux Mir-Lelith.

The human, who fenced all manner of contraband within the sector, was as hard to read as Vic himself. Only, he wasn't a cyborg.

Vic was always relieved when he walked away from a transaction with Crux without having to draw his laser-pistol.

"Good idea," he replied. "Let's get ready … although we won't unload the cargo until I've been paid." Crux had been delighted to hear he could source this merch and had promised to pay him incredibly well for it, but Vic would only relax when he had those hard credits on his device.

# 6. GETTING DOWN TO BUSINESS

EMERGING FROM A shop, Aria caught a glimpse of her reflection in the one-way glass outside.

A tall, voluptuous woman clad in a deep violet quilted jacket and flowing pants stared back at her.

Aria's mouth quirked. She'd meant to go shopping for underwear only, but since she'd been wearing that wine-red jumpsuit for the past three days, she decided to buy a fresh set of clothing as well. She'd managed to stuff the jumpsuit into her backpack and would see about laundering it back on Vic's ship. She still wore her purple cloak though. It didn't need washing as often as the rest of her clothing, and she didn't want to swap it for another shade.

As a Haliaen native, Aria favored flamboyant, brightly-hued clothes. Purple was her, and her father's, favorite color.

The reminder of Morgan Mir-Straken made her smile fade. She'd thought about contacting him, to let him know she was alive and well, after fleeing Haliaen, but had quickly dismissed the impulse. The clan-lord wouldn't be worried about her right now. Instead, he'd be fuming. Her father had worked to create a blood-tie between the Mir-Strakens and the Mir-Ferrins for years, and in one move, she'd destroyed all his plans.

He'd never forgive her for that.

"Sorry dad," she murmured. "There are some lines I won't cross."

Pushing aside thoughts of the man she'd never understood, Aria squared her shoulders and glanced around her. She stood in the midst of a mall: terraces of shops wrapped around a cavernous atrium. Silver Mir-Lelith banners stretched between pillars, while a glass roof arched above her, letting in silvery daylight. Snow swirled in the pale sky, a reminder of the sub-zero temperatures outdoors. Inside, however, the air was pleasantly warm.

Aria had shopped as quickly as she could, but she had to move on now.

*Time to be getting back to the ship.*

She made her way down the walkway, while the bland tinkle of piped-in music flowed through the mall. Along the way, she passed tiny shrines to the various galactic gods. Among all the clans, the Mir-Leliths were the most devout. Incense and candles burned in the neat alcoves, and she passed a few cloaked individuals who knelt before the shrines, heads bent in prayer.

Aria headed toward the nearest transpod station. Sleek silver bullets sped through the tunnels that coiled around the exterior of the vast city. Fort Elisik was truly massive; the transpod journey from the landing bay to the nearest shopping mall had taken her over thirty minutes.

Glancing down at the display on her wrist-comm, which she'd adjusted to local time as soon as they landed, Aria's brow furrowed. She needed to get back to *The Wayfarer*.

She approached the transpod station, where a crowd of cloaked shoppers had already gathered, awaiting the next departure. She joined them. Moments later, the transpod arrived, and they piled on. The pods here were nearly three times the size of those on Lanthor—long and streamlined rather than spherical. They were big enough to have two aisles of seats and three sets of doors.

Most of the seats were taken, so Aria squeezed in next to one of the exterior windows and grabbed hold of the railing as the transpod whispered out of the station, beginning its wide, spiraling descent to the lower levels. Like on the way up, it traveled down a transparent tunnel that hugged the conical surface of Fort Elisik. From her vantage point, Aria gazed out through the glass and swirling snow, across the icy tundra.

The journey was slow, for they stopped every few minutes to let off passengers and acquire new ones. Despite that she was eager to return to the landing bay, Aria found herself enjoying the ride. The view was starkly beautiful, and the journey gave her time to reflect on the events of the past days.

Her thoughts then turned to Vic.

There was no doubt about it; he was easily the most interesting individual she'd ever crossed paths with. She was grateful he'd offered to take her to Staturine II; nonetheless, she felt bad about involving him in her situation. She'd caused him a lot of trouble back on Lanthor.

The transpod slid to a halt at one of the many stops then, the doors whispering open. Emerging from her thoughts about her unlikely hero, Aria watched a group of pilgrims flood onto the pod—followers of Wis, the Seer of Truth. Wearing shimmering black robes, their heads shaved, they silently filed into the pod. The scent of incense wafted through the space.

Beyond the transpod platform, a wide atrium opened up, and towering black spires thrust skyward from its center.

Aria's mouth tugged into a smile at the magnificent sight. Of course, Fort Elisik was home to the biggest shrine to Wis in the Rith sector. The Seer of Truth was a popular god on her world too; there were shrines to him on nearly every street corner, but the most pious acolytes made the pilgrimage to Fort Elisik.

A pang went through her then, her chest tightening as memories flooded back. After her mother had died, she'd taken to visiting their local shrine and lighting incense. Marie Mir-Straken had been a devout follower. She'd told her daughter that Wis saw all, right into the hearts of every galactic soul.

Staying true to him kept you on the right path.

Aria would have liked to visit the temple and light a stick of incense while she closed her eyes and remembered her mother—but she had to get back to the ship.

Leaning against the railing, Aria shifted her attention from the view beyond the transpod station. Her gaze slid over the last of the passengers that were getting on from the crowded platform.

Amongst them, she spied a flash of bronze.

Vic clenched his jaw and zig-zagged his way through the press of black-robed bodies. Pilgrims were everywhere, their solemn faces turned toward the looming temple. Even from this street, which led from the transpod station to the great atrium beyond, the Temple to Wis was impossible to miss.

Shaped like a crown, with rows of needle-sharp black spires, it was fashioned out of gleaming obsidian. Up ahead, Vic spied rows of acolytes prostrating themselves before the tear-drop-shaped entrance to the temple. Despite the crowds, it was surprisingly quiet on this level.

Wis valued silence.

Huffing a sigh, Vic wished his client had chosen somewhere else to meet. There must be a festival to Wis on at present, for he'd never seen so many pilgrims in one place. The overpowering scent of incense was making Vic's nose itch.

He'd never been a follower of any of the gods. Having grown up in a military family, with a father who served the Mir-Ferrins with a religious-like zeal, Vic had learned from an early age to put his faith in only himself. His father had given his life for the Mir-Ferrins, and Vic had nearly gone the same way.

In his opinion, religion was for the weak-minded.

Cutting through the crowd, Vic scanned the row of eateries that flanked one side of the street. A wide overhang shadowed their entrances. He'd arranged to meet his client on the terrace of a tearoom. Crux wanted to sit inside, but Vic had insisted they conducted business outdoors.

The past years had taught him it was best to meet somewhere relatively public, just in case negotiations turned nasty. Crux's bodyguards weren't likely to pull a gun on him with an audience.

Spying his destination, *The Blizzard Tea House*, Vic cast a glance over his shoulder. Obsidian stood just behind him, its gaze surveying the press of robed figures surrounding them. However, Vic marked how the pilgrims gave them both a wide berth.

Crowds always tended to part for a cyborg and a battle-droid.

"Come on," he murmured to Obsidian. "It's over there … I see Crux and his minders."

The human rose to his feet as Vic approached the tearoom's terrace. Tall, suave, and dressed in flowing sky-blue robes, Crux Mir-Lelith looked like a politician rather than someone who fenced stolen goods. His blond hair was neatly styled, and his skin deeply tanned, at odds with this planet's freezing climate.

A charming smile stretched Crux's mouth as Vic drew near—an expression that didn't warm his blue eyes.

It was one of the reasons Vic had never trusted him.

"Vic!" Crux welcomed him. "How about all these damn pilgrims, eh? Fort Elisik will end up overrun at this rate."

Vic gave a non-committal grunt in reply. He wasn't one for small-talk.

Crux didn't extend a hand to greet him. They'd never shaken on any of the deals they'd made. Vic imagined, like many people, Crux didn't wish to touch a cyborg.

That suited him just fine.

Two grey-scaled Rendak flanked Crux. They were both as tall and lanky as Obsidian, with flat faces and deep-set eyes that rested upon Vic and his companion. Thin tongues flicked out of lipless mouths, tasting the air around them. Both Rendak wore laser-pistols at their hips.

Unease flickered through Vic. Crux always met him with his bodyguards in tow, but there was something about the keen way they'd tracked his path toward the terrace that made his hackles rise. He was wary of Rendak; they were cunning and vicious in a fight. The pirate who'd shot him in the chest years earlier had been a Rendak.

"Good day, Crux," Vic replied. He pulled out a chair and slid into it, while Obsidian rattled to a halt at his shoulder.

His client called the server-droid that was waiting tables over. "I'll have a pot of Mandalian Purple Leaf," he said before casting a look over at Vic.

"Certainly," the squat droid bleeped, swiveling to Vic. "And you, Sir?"

"Nothing for me, thanks," Vic replied. There wasn't any point in drawing this meeting out. He wanted to conclude business and get off this frozen planet so that Jenna Mir-Brennan could learn about what the Mir-Ferrins were planning.

Crux arched an eyebrow. "You don't enjoy tea, Captain?"

"Not especially."

Crux settled back into his chair, adjusting the long sleeves of his costly robe. "Very well." His gaze speared Vic's. "You have the parts then?"

Vic nodded.

"Do you know their origin?"

"They're Mir-Straken."

"Are they equipped with Felda Magnets?"

"Of course ... I assured you they'd be the latest technology."

Crux's tea arrived then upon a gleaming platter. The droid placed the teapot and cup before its customer and was about to pour when he waved it away. "I'll take care of that."

"Yes, Sir," the droid chirped, backing off.

Crux picked up the teapot and carefully poured steaming purple liquid into a small cup.

Vic watched him, impatience curling within him.

Why did his clients take so long over doing business? Many of them treated these meetings like social engagements. Crux wasn't a man to rush anything.

Fortunately, just like when he'd negotiated with the Vulkar back on Lanthor, Vic's irritation wouldn't be showing.

"Five hyperdrives," Vic said eventually when the silence stretched out. "All brand-new, ready to be installed. That'll be fifteen hundred credits, as agreed."

Crux smiled. "In a hurry today, Captain?"

Vic didn't reply.

Crux lifted his delicate cup to his lips and took a sip. "Mir-Straken hyperdrives are likely worth that to me … but I won't be paying you a single credit." He paused then, his blue eyes glinting. "Instead, you're going to give that merch to me … for free."

# 7. INTO THE DARK

SILENCE STRETCHED BETWEEN them before Vic finally spoke. "And why would I do that?"

The smile remained upon Crux's lips as he took another sip of tea, although his gaze turned as sharp as glass. "Because that shipment of detonator fuses I paid you a thousand credits for five months ago was faulty. I've had several unhappy clients demanding refunds ever since."

Vic's pulse quickened. *Shit.* He'd bought those fuses on Idral, from a source he didn't usually work with. He'd had a bad feeling about the man when they'd shaken on the deal, but in the passing months hadn't given it much thought.

He should have known it would come back to bite him.

Feigning nonchalance, Vic leaned back in his seat and folded his arms across his chest. "My client assured me they were high quality."

"Well, they weren't … and I want compensating." Crux's smile tightened. "Reputation is everything in this business … you know that."

Vic did. He'd worked hard to build his own. However, Crux Mir-Lelith was influential in the circles they moved in.

Damn it though, he didn't want to hand over those hyperdrives for free. After the rescue mission to Idral a year earlier, *The Wayfarer* had been out of action for three months—and he hadn't been earning in that time. He'd been playing catch-up ever since. Jenna Mir-Brennan had paid him well for the mission, but he'd had a few debts to repay. Fuel was expensive, as were the numerous tolls to use the fastest shipping lanes.

He needed those credits to pay for his next shipment of merch.

"Come on, Crux … I dealt with you in good faith," he said, spreading his hands in a placating gesture. "I'd never *knowingly* sell you defective merch."

Crux's mouth quirked. "Indeed, I've always thought you a man of your word, Mir-Riorde … and that's why you're going to do the right thing now."

They stared at each other.

Vic's pulse quickened further. "I'll give you the hyperdrives for half price."

Crux's gaze narrowed. He raised a lazy hand, gesturing to his bodyguards. "No … you'll hand them over gratis. I'll send Corl and Wrel down to the landing bays now to unload the drives." He paused then. "Don't give us any trouble."

Heat ignited under Vic's ribcage. He didn't take kindly to threats. And he didn't like being backed into a corner either.

He hadn't lied to Crux; the dealer on Idral had assured him the detonator fuses were all in working order. He'd even tested one out for Vic.

*What if Crux is lying to me?*

The heat spread to Vic's gut. He lowered his hands, sliding them under the table. His laser-pistol was within easy reach, and he was a quick draw. However, he didn't want to get into a fight here. The Mir-Lelith garrisons were some of the harshest in the sector. He'd already seen a few patrols of hard-faced guards clad in silver armor patrolling the loading bays and transpod routes of the city. He didn't feel like having to explain himself to them, or being locked up in a Mir-Lelith detention center for killing one of their citizens.

A tense silence fell. Crux had abandoned his tea now and was watching Vic with a hooded gaze.

Gasps and murmurs intruded then.

Vic tore his attention from his client and glanced right, across the stream of pilgrims moving along the street, traveling to and from the transpod station.

And there, cleaving a path through the crowd, were four bronze battle-droids.

The fire in Vic's gut extinguished, and he breathed a curse.

"Excuse me?" Crux snapped. A pause followed as the dealer's gaze followed Vic's. "What are Mir-Ferrin battle-droids doing here?"

Indeed, battle-droids were a rare sight in this corner of the sector. Obsidian always drew stares whenever they traded away from Mir-Ferrin planets, despite that its black armor stood him apart from these ones.

But Vic knew why they were here, and whom they were hunting.

"We'll have to conclude this conversation later," he announced, rising to his feet.

"No, we won't." The charm had drained from Crux's voice. His tanned face was taut and his usually smooth brow creased. "This isn't up for discussion. You're handing over those hyperdrives to me. Today. For free."

Vic didn't answer.

He vaulted over the railing and dove into the press of black-robed figures. He didn't ask Obsidian to follow, for he knew the droid would.

Vic's gaze swept his surroundings, searching for Aria.

An instant later, he saw her.

Aria must have run straight by him seconds earlier, yet he hadn't seen her. She fled toward the atrium now. Chestnut hair flew behind her, her purple cloak billowing, as she elbowed her way through the throng.

"Fuck," Vic breathed. This was the last thing he needed right now. He then shouted, "Aria!"

Her gaze jerked his way. A moment later, he'd exited the street and was at her side, hauling her with him as they headed toward a row of bars on the opposite side of the atrium.

"I thought you were grabbing a few items and heading back to the ship," he ground out, shoving a pilgrim out of the way.

"That was the plan," she muttered. "But I was on a transpod heading back to the landing bay when the battle-droids got on. I had to get off before they caught me. Gods, how did they get here so fast?"

Vic wondered that himself. Glancing over his shoulder, he spied Obsidian loping along behind them. The battle-droid had unslung a laser-rifle from over its shoulder. At the sight of the armed droid, the crowd scattered, cries of fright lifting high into the atrium.

A few yards behind Obsidian, the Mir-Ferrin battle-droids were closing in fast.

"How are we getting out of here?" Aria glanced around, her expression taut. "They'll catch us if we try to jump on a transpod."

Vic clenched his teeth. No, that wouldn't work for them this time. His gaze flicked over their surroundings, his mind working fast, churning over possibilities. He came up with none.

"Maybe we can lose them in the temple," Aria said then, her fingernails digging into his arm. "There must be a back entrance of some kind."

Vic nodded. Scanning his surroundings, his gaze alighted upon the crown of gleaming black spires rearing up before them. The temple wasn't a great option, but he didn't have a better idea. "Let's go."

They veered right, back into the crowd, shoving their way to where followers knelt before the entrance.

"Sincere apologies," Aria murmured while Vic shoved acolytes out of the way to gain access. "I'm really sorry about this."

"Stop apologizing," he growled.

"I can't help it," she shot back. "This is sacrilegious."

"Better that than get caught." Vic let go of Aria's arm and stormed into the temple, drawing his laser-pistol as he went.

Inside, it was dimly lit and echoey, with no natural light entering except through the open doorway. The air was thick with cloying incense. Banks of flickering candles illuminated the cavernous space. A row of pilgrims queued before the altar, waiting for their turn to light a stick of incense and whisper prayers to their dead.

Above them stood a high statue of Wis the Seer himself:
a robed figure wearing a serene expression, his arms
spread in a benevolent gesture.

"This way." Vic skirted the edge of the circular
temple, past rows of candles.

The thunder of heavy feet behind them warned Vic
that they hadn't lost their pursuers.

"They're gaining on us, Vic." Obsidian's rasp reached
him then.

Whipping around, Vic raised his laser-pistol.

"No!" Aria gasped. "Don't shoot … not in here!"

Vic ignored her and began firing on the battle-droids.
Next to him, Obsidian raised his laser-rifle and followed
suit. The roar of discharging laser bolts echoed
obscenely through the cavernous space, tearing through
the reverent silence.

Gasps and cries followed from the pilgrims gathered
near the altar, and Aria whispered a prayer under her
breath, begging for forgiveness from Wis himself.

Vic clenched his jaw and opened fire once more.
Prayers weren't going to get them out of here.

Interestingly, their pursuers didn't fire back.

The Mir-Ferrin clan-lord didn't want his fiancée
injured.

Vic and Obsidian's fire barely made a dent in the
battle-droids' armor, although that wasn't surprising.
Nonetheless, they managed to bring a chandelier of
candles down on the droids, giving the three of them a
chance to get away once more.

Vic, Aria, and Obsidian crashed through a door at the
back of the nave and into a long dining hall, barreling
through a group of robed priests who were carrying
platters of food from the kitchen.

Screams assaulted Vic's ears, but he kept going.
Maybe the kitchen would lead them through to a rear
exit.

Unlike the dimly lit temple, the kitchens were so
bright it made his eye sting. Utility-droids of all shapes
and sizes filled the space, stirring pots and dicing

vegetables at long benches. A few of them let out shrill squeals of alarm at the sight of the three intruders. The sound of dropping lids and whirring, as the droids moved out of the way, echoed through the steamy air.

"Look … a freight elevator!" Aria panted. "We can use it to get off this level." She headed to where a gleaming metal panel sat at the far end of the kitchen.

Vic reluctantly followed. It wasn't the exit he'd anticipated. He didn't like the thought of jamming himself into a freight elevator—they were meant for cargo, not life forms—it would be too much like that claustrophobic pod he'd slept inside on the Mir-Ferrin battleship after his transitioning. Nonetheless, their alternatives right now were few.

Reaching the panel, Aria grabbed hold of a handle at the bottom and yanked upward.

To Vic's relief, the elevator was decently-sized—big enough to bring in trolleys of supplies from the lower levels. He and Aria could stand upright without their heads brushing the roof, yet Obsidian had to bend double to get inside.

Vic leaned out and punched the button next to the elevator before yanking his arm inside. With a jolt, the elevator started to move. There was no time to pull the door down. As they dropped, Vic caught sight of their pursuers crashing through the kitchen.

An instant later, they were descending into darkness.

# 8. TO THEIR MERCY

ARIA LEANED AGAINST the cold wall of the freight elevator, breathing hard.

They'd lost the battle-droids for the moment, yet had left chaos in their wake. When she'd suggested that they escape their pursuers in the temple, she hadn't thought Vic would crash through it firing his laser-pistol. He'd dishonored the sacred space. He didn't seem to care, but she did.

An eerie crimson light illuminated the elevator, preventing it from being shrouded in utter darkness. An instant later, Aria realized it was coming from Obsidian's red eyes. The light was stark, highlighting the taut angles of Vic's face. The cyborg's jaw was clenched, his eye narrowed. He looked seriously pissed off.

"Are you mad at me?" she asked. "I was trying to get back to the ship, you know, I wasn't—"

"You're not to blame," he cut her off gruffly. "I'm annoyed with myself ... if I hadn't made this detour here, we wouldn't be in this mess."

They plummeted downward, dropping so fast that Aria had to brace herself against the surrounding walls to steady herself—before the service elevator jerked to a halt.

The movement was so abrupt that Aria stumbled forward, straight into Vic's arms. He caught her as she slammed into the hard wall of his chest. Her hand went up to brace herself, and her left palm felt the cold, hard plate that covered the right side of his chest.

An instant later, the elevator started lifting.

Aria's heart leaped into her throat. The battle-droids had overridden the controls and were calling them back.

Vic growled a curse and gently pushed Aria away from him, setting her on her feet. His gaze flicked upward then, and he glanced over at Obsidian. "Can you deal with this?"

The battle-droid swiveled, its clawed hand yanking off the metal plate on the wall. It then delved through a spiderweb of wiring and stuck its finger into a socket.

The elevator jerked to a halt once more—and then they were plummeting earthward again. On the way, they passed several doors, which presumably led out onto different kitchens on the various levels below the one they'd escaped from.

Aria stumbled, backward this time, and braced herself against the walls of the elevator.

Better Vic didn't catch her fall. The hard strength of his body, and the heat the emanated from him, did alarming things to her already racing pulse.

Obsidian kept its finger jammed into the socket until they came to a shuddering halt on the bottom of the shaft. The droid then extracted its hand from the sparking panel, and moved to the door, before reaching down and yanking it upward.

The screech of protesting metal followed.

Aria followed her companions out into a shadowy warehouse. Towering pallets of food supplies formed high walls on either side, while utility-droids driving forklifts and platform carts trundled past.

Vic and Aria's heavy boots echoed loudly in the vast space, as did the thump of Obsidian's rubber-soled feet. Aria kept glancing behind her, expecting to see battle-droids erupt from the empty freight elevator—however, they'd bought themselves some time.

They needed to use it.

Reaching the exit to the warehouse, they entered a huge market. The musky scent of ripe fruit and the metallic tang of fresh meat drifted over them, as did the chatter of voices as vendors and shoppers haggled for the best price.

Lined by wide windows on one side that looked over snow-covered tundra, the market consisted of row upon row of brightly colored stalls. The floor glistened wet, hosed down by a trundling droid. The eye-watering smell of detergent caught in the back of Aria's throat, making her cough.

She hurried after Vic and Obsidian. Usually, she'd have lingered in such a place, enjoying the unfamiliar sights and sounds of the liveliest market she'd ever seen. Right now, all she could think about was running.

All the same, the market was too colorful and vibrant to ignore completely. She passed a Nandoon haggling with a vendor selling massive pink-speckled eggs. The shopper was getting agitated, her wattles quivering as the egg seller refused to lower his price.

A chill swept over Aria then. It didn't matter where she went or how far she ran, the battle-droids were never more than two steps behind her.

*I'll never outrun them.*

Reaching a transpod station on the far side of the market, she stepped close to Vic and plucked at his sleeve to catch his attention. "Vic … how far away is the landing bay?"

Vic swiveled, his gaze spearing hers. They were standing close, near enough for her to note that his hazel eye had flecks of gold and green through it. "Don't worry," he said roughly. "It's a short ride from here."

Once again, she sensed his simmering anger. However, unlike when they'd been in the freight elevator, she didn't question him about it. Clearly, he was still wrestling with his conscience about bringing her here. She too wished he'd left this job until afterward.

Passengers poured off the incoming transpod, a flood of robed figures carrying shopping baskets, and then Aria followed her two companions inside.

Lowering herself to a seat, for her legs were suddenly shaky, she pulled up the cowl of her cloak. Vic and Obsidian remained standing, two silent sentinels behind her.

The transpod departed, sliding out of the station and winding its way up toward the landing bays. The pod rapidly filled up, and every time they slid into a station, Aria's pulse raced.

Being hunted would turn her into a nervous wreck. She was starting to jump at shadows.

Approaching the landing bay doors, Vic had the presence of mind to draw his laser-pistol. He'd spent the transpod journey silently berating himself, not only for making this detour, but also for not questioning why Crux Mir-Lelith had offered such a high sum for those hyperdrives. The cheating bastard had never intended to pay for them, but Vic had let greed override good sense. He'd made a serious misstep—one that could have cost him his life.

*I'm losing my touch.*

Vic couldn't dwell on his mistakes now. They weren't out of trouble yet—he needed to keep focused.

Jaw clenched, he heard the scrape of steel behind him as Obsidian drew his weapon. And when Vic stepped inside the landing bay, he was glad they had.

Corl and Wrel were waiting for him, flanked by four other Rendak. Forming a row in front of *The Wayfarer*, all six of them had guns, and when Vic and his companions stepped into the hangar, they raised them.

Aria gasped and came to an abrupt halt, twisting to flee, but Vic grabbed hold of her arm, steadying her.

"Don't run … I was worried we might have company."

"But who are they?" she hissed back.

"They work for the client I was meeting here."

Corl stepped forward, leveling his laser-pistol at Vic's chest. "Going somewhere, Mir-Riorde?"

"I *was*, actually," Vic replied, his voice toneless. Both he and Obsidian had their weapons pointed at Crux's bodyguards. It wouldn't be an easy fight—two against six armed Rendak, but he'd had worse odds. Battle-droids and cyborgs were difficult to bring down—even against Rendak—and Crux knew it.

Corl's slender tongue darted out, his deep-set eyes flicking to where Aria stood at Vic's shoulder. "Using your lady friend as an excuse to run out on a client is bad form … Crux isn't happy."

Vic's jaw tightened, although he remained stubbornly silent.

"We can do this the hard way or the easy way," Wrel added, with a thin smile. "Open up the hold and let us take what you owe Crux, and there's no need to shed any blood."

Vic still didn't answer. He sensed Aria's tension next to him. The lie in Wrel's voice was evident. Once he opened the cargo hold and let the Rendak take the hyperdrives, they'd shoot him and her in the head.

It would be messy and public, especially since other ships used this landing bay, and there were security cameras everywhere, but Vic wouldn't be surprised if Crux had the Fort Elisik governor in his pocket.

They'd look the other way.

Corl's mouth twitched, although his gaze remained steady. "Come on, Captain, we don't have time for games."

The whoosh of opening doors behind them made Vic glance over his shoulder.

His breath caught at the sight of four bronze battle-droids marching into the loading bay, laser-rifles aloft.

In an instant, he knew how they were getting out of this.

"Move," he grunted to Obsidian. He then grabbed hold of Aria's arm, hauling her against him as he dove left. Despite that he'd surprised her, she recovered well, letting her body relax into the roll he went into.

Detonating laser bolts echoed through the hangar.

As Vic had hoped, the Rendak were trigger-happy—and the battle-droids had caught them off-guard.

The battle-droids returned fire, while Vic rolled to his feet, bringing Aria with him. She was a tall, well-built woman, but his transitioning had augmented his strength, and he picked her up easily.

He then pushed her behind them as they edged along the far wall toward the nose of his freighter.

One of the Rendak whipped around to fire on him, but Vic was quicker, shooting him in the throat.

Meanwhile, Obsidian plowed headlong into the fray, knocking two of Crux's bodyguards out of the way to reach the hatch.

Vic edged closer, although with more caution than his first mate. He didn't have plate armor like Obsidian.

The battle-droids had been reluctant to use their weapons with Aria nearby earlier, but now faced with Rendak, they opened fire. The stench of burning flesh wafted across the landing bay as Wrel crumpled.

The remaining four Rendak moved forward, drawing laser-blades to engage the battle-droids at close quarters—and Vic seized his opportunity. The blades flashed white as they turned them to the 'kill' setting.

Vic's hand grasped Aria's, and he pulled her with him, reaching *The Wayfarer* and sliding along the ship's side to where Obsidian waited.

As he approached, Vic nodded to his copilot.

Obsidian punched in a code, and the hatch opened, the ramp lowering with a hiss.

Corl whirled from having severed the head of a battle-droid with his laser-blade. The weapon's hum echoed against the surrounding steel. Glowing white blade still held aloft, the Rendak's flat face twisted, and he dove for Vic.

He never reached him.

Obsidian raised his laser-rifle and shot Corl in the left flank. The Rendak lurched sideways, crumpling onto the metal floor.

A moment later, Vic, Aria, and Obsidian were inside *The Wayfarer,* and Vic slammed his hand down on the button next to the hatch.

The ramp rose, and as it did, Vic watched Corl roll onto his back, clutching his side. Dark blood seeped through his fingers, but his flat eyes were fixed upon Vic.

The door sealed, and Vic followed Obsidian through to the cockpit.

He fired up the engines, flicking switches and adjusting instruments, before glancing over his shoulder.

He was going to tell Aria to strap herself in, but there was no need.

She was already seated, harness clipped on.

Turning back to the instrument panel, Vic nodded to Obsidian. "Raise the shields … we're starting to make a habit of these sudden departures."

# 9. BUGGED

THEY DIDN'T SPEAK until *The Wayfarer* had broken free of Calberic's orbit, until Vic had charted a path, found a lane to Staturine II, and made the jump into hyperspace.

Even then, Aria was wary of distracting her pilot.

They'd shot out of that landing bay in Fort Elisik, scattering the two battle-droids who'd been firing at the cockpit windows, and roared out into a blizzard. As when they'd fled from Lanthor, the comms console in the cockpit had gone berserk, bleeping hysterically.

Vic didn't answer it.

Now that they were in hyperspace, the bleeping had stopped.

Aria unclipped her harness and rose to her feet. She then cleared her throat. "Does this mean you'll get another fine?"

"Most likely," Vic replied. He still had his back to her as he checked the instruments. "But that's the least of my worries."

Silence followed this admission before Aria finally broke it. "Why did the Rendak want to steal your cargo?"

Vic turned then, his gaze settling on her. "Their boss decided he was owed." He rose from his seat with the loose-limbed grace she'd noted in him from their first meeting and stepped down from the cockpit. "I'm sorry, Aria … making that stop was selfish of me … especially with so much at stake."

Aria's mouth lifted at the corners. "Apology accepted." She then gave a rueful shake of her head. "Don't be too hard on yourself. You weren't to know those battle-droids would catch up with us so fast."

"There's only one reason they did," he replied, his voice lowering. "They're tracking you."

Aria arched her eyebrows. "What? How?"

"Did you turn the geo-locator off on your tablet … your wrist-comm?"

"Of course," she replied, affronted that he'd think she was that stupid. "It was the first thing I did before I even left Haliaen."

Vic crossed his arms then. "Well, that only leaves one alternative … someone has put a tracking device on you."

Cold swept over Aria, and she glanced down at the backpack she'd just shrugged off. "That's impossible," she whispered.

"Let's find out, shall we?" Vic crossed to a locker next to the bunks and opened it, before pulling out a palm-sized, spoon-shaped metal device. "I'll check you out with a bug-sweeper."

Aria moved to the back of the cabin. Placing the backpack on the table, she opened it and poured out its contents on the table. "Go on then," she muttered, irritation bubbling up now. "But I don't think you'll have any luck."

Switching on the bug-sweeper, which emitted a high-pitched hum, Vic approached the table. Firstly, he picked up the empty bag and scanned it.

"That's clean, at least," he murmured.

Aria looked on as he ran the sweeper over all her possessions—few as they were—checking for bugs. He picked up her tablet and scanned it carefully before working his way through the other contents.

He even scanned the wrapped nutri-bars, her jumpsuit, which was badly in need of a wash, and the underwear she'd just bought.

Aria's cheeks started to burn when he ran the sweeper over a pair of sheer black panties. Thank the Gods she had gotten into the habit of throwing away used underwear—there was no time to do laundry when you were on the run—buying new items as she went. She wasn't enjoying this forced intimacy.

Vic didn't appear to be either, for he finished the rest of his sweep quickly.

And as she'd predicted, his search of her bag yielded nothing.

Stepping back from the table, Vic turned to her. "Your turn."

Aria inclined her head. "Excuse me?"

"There's a tracking device somewhere, Aria. And if it's not among your possessions, it'll be on you."

She folded her arms across her chest. "This is ridiculous."

"Maybe … but since you're on my ship, I insist."

Her gaze narrowed, and she lapsed into stubborn silence. Moments passed, and it became clear he wasn't going to back down. Eventually, Aria huffed an irritated sigh. "Go on then."

"Stand with your legs apart, and with your arms raised," he instructed.

Aria's cheeks, which had just started to cool, burned hot again. She was grateful her coppery skin masked the depth of her embarrassment.

Vic stepped close and began to sweep the scanner over her. The bug-sweeper crackled as he passed it down her neck and her arms.

Standing this close, Aria caught the spicy scent of Vic's skin, blended with the faint scent of the bodywash he'd used the last time he showered. He smelled good, and as when she'd fallen into his arms in the freight elevator, his nearness overwhelmed her senses.

Closing her eyes, she willed him to hurry up and finish his bug sweep.

*He'll never find anything*, she told herself. He was right—it was incredible that wherever she went, the battle-droids turned up within hours—but there had to be another explanation.

Elijah had sent his henchmen, and as clan-lord, he had access to the latest technology. You usually couldn't track a ship once it made the jump into hyperspace, but perhaps they could.

The bug-sweeper let out a shrill 'bleep' then, and Aria started, her eyes flying open. "What—"

"Hold still." Vic was standing behind her. "I need to be sure."

Another accusatory 'bleep' echoed through the cabin, so loud that Obsidian twisted in its seat in the cockpit, its gaze settling upon her.

"It's in your lower back," Vic said after a brief pause. "Just to the right of your spine."

Aria's skin started to prickle, queasiness rising. "The bug-sweeper must be faulty," she whispered. "I think I'd know if anyone planted a bug *in* me." Unlike earlier, her voice wasn't quite as confident.

Instead, she felt as if her world was unraveling, even more than it already had.

"Have you undergone any surgery lately?" Vic asked, his voice practical, clipped. She was grateful for his calmness, for her pulse quickened.

"Yes," she whispered. "My father insisted I have my eggs harvested."

A pause followed before Vic spoke once more. "You're a bit young for that, aren't you?"

"I'm twenty-six, but fertility issues run in my family … the egg harvesting was insurance, just in case I have trouble conceiving after my marriage."

Aria didn't like discussing this with Vic; it was too personal. Her father's insistence had angered her. As his only child, he'd always been paranoid that the Mir-Straken ruling line would be lost. He planned that one of her children would rule their clan one day and didn't wish to take any chances. His attitude had made Aria feel used, treated like a breeding machine.

Swallowing hard, she forced herself to focus on the present.

"They didn't put me under general anesthetic for the procedure though … and I don't remember the doctor going anywhere near my back."

Vic moved around to face her, their gazes meeting. "Are you sure about that?"

Aria's heart started to hammer, her palms turning sweaty. Casting her mind back, she recalled dozing during the procedure, which was strange since she'd been anxious beforehand. Dozing wasn't the same as falling asleep—yet suddenly, she couldn't be as vehement as earlier. "No," she replied softly. "I'm not."

"I've got some anesthetic in here." Vic opened the medic kit, studying the contents. "Do you want me to numb the area?"

"Best not." Aria's voice was low, subdued. "It's near my spine ... a bit risky."

Her voice was tense, brittle.

He didn't blame her. Someone, most likely her father, had put a tracker in her without her permission.

"All right," Vic murmured. "I'll put some ice on the skin first though ... to ease the pain a little." He glanced over at where his first mate had emerged from the cockpit to watch. "Fetch me some ice from the dispenser, Obsidian."

The battle-droid gave a nod and moved off to do as bid.

Aria lay on her stomach on the bottom bunk in the berth, the quilted jacket and shirt she wore underneath pulled up to reveal her naked back. Once Obsidian brought the ice, Vic shifted closer to Aria, kneeling next to the bunk, and reaching out to touch the spot that had caused the bug-sweeper to go off.

"Can you feel anything?" Aria asked.

Gently prodding with his index finger, Vic located something small and hard. "Yes ... it's not too far under the skin."

Aria let out a shaky laugh. "Thank Syr the Merciful for that."

"Okay ... I'm going to numb the area with some ice," Vic said, taking the cup of ice cubes Obsidian passed him.

"Go ahead."

Reaching out, Vic gently tugged the waistband of her cargos down a little, to give himself more space to work.

However, he immediately regretted the action when it revealed a dimple above the lush swell of her buttocks.

Vic froze, his breathing growing shallow as his groin stiffened.

Arousal was the last thing he needed right now. When Aria had fallen into his arms in the freight elevator, the feel of her softness against him had made his heart kick against his ribs.

*Focus.*

Trying to ignore the press of his cock against his pants, Vic extracted three ice cubes and placed them upon her lower back, to the right of her spine.

"I'll just leave them there for a minute or two," he explained, sitting back on his heels.

"Okay," she whispered back.

Silence settled then—tense and awkward. Vic cleared his throat. "Do you have any idea why your father would have you bugged?"

"None." Her voice was barely above a whisper.

"Didn't he trust you?"

"I thought he did … but I'm beginning to think otherwise." He heard the resentment in her tone—an emotion he knew well. In the first years after his desertion, it had been his constant companion, simmering in his gut. He'd given his life to the Mir-Ferrin space fleet, but after the transitioning went wrong, he'd realized what a waste it had all been.

He'd signed his free will away without a thought. He wasn't a Mir-Ferrin, yet his clan, the Mir-Riordes, had always served them. His father had gone to his grave with unwavering loyalty.

"Maybe father worried I didn't intend to go through with the marriage to Elijah," Aria admitted then, her shoulders tensing. "I can't believe he'd plant a tracking device on me though."

"Well, someone did." Vic removed the ice cubes and reached for a paper towel to pat dry her skin. Fortunately, his erection was starting to subside; he didn't need the distraction. "Perhaps your fiancé is behind it."

Aria snorted. "Elijah isn't the possessive type … we don't have that kind of relationship. We were childhood friends, not lovers." She broke off as if realizing she'd been too candid. "Of course, that was going to change after the wedding."

Vic reached into the medic kit and retrieved a scalpel. Stripping off its protective covering, he attached it to a handle. "Right," he murmured, shifting close to Aria once more. "I'll try and do this fast." He cast a glance left at where the battle-droid looked on. "Obsidian … grab some paper towels to staunch the bleeding."

"I'm ready," Aria assured him. Her voice, although tense, was resolute. "Do it."

Vic brought the scalpel down and made an incision across the top of the bug. Aria inhaled sharply, yet he didn't halt. Once the first incision was complete, he made another, forming a cross.

Blood started to well, but Vic paid it no mind for the moment. Instead, he plucked a sterilized pair of tweezers out of the medic kit. Folding back the skin with the tip of his scalpel, he caught sight of something small and metallic, glinting in the stark cabin light. "There it is," he muttered. He inserted the tweezers into the wound, placing the flat of his hand on the small of Aria's back to steady her.

Under his palm, he could feel the light sheen of sweat and the tension that shivered through her.

An instant later though, he'd plucked the bug out of her flesh, and he held it aloft. "Got it."

Vic then took the paper towels from Obsidian and placed them upon the wound, holding them firm with his left hand while he held the object up to the light and examined it. Even coated in blood, he recognized the device. "That's a bug all right," he murmured. "An expensive one."

# 10. A GOOD MAN

"HOLD STILL … I'M just putting some plasti-skin over the wound."

Gritting her teeth, Aria nodded.

Vic had already put some antiseptic on the incisions he'd made, and her lower back now felt as if it were on fire.

"There, done."

Aria pushed herself gingerly up and swiveled around into a sitting position, pulling her top down as she went. The burning pain in her back had now settled into a dull throb. She didn't mind the pain though; it distracted her from the tang of betrayal that soured her mouth.

If she'd thought her life was unraveling earlier, it now felt as if her entire existence had just been turned upside down. Someone had planted a bug in her back—and that *someone* was likely to be her father.

Her chest started to ache then. *How could he?* She couldn't believe he had such little respect for her.

When she eventually spoke, her voice was subdued, husky. "Can I see the bug?"

Vic glanced up from where he was kneeling next to the bed, putting away items into the medic kit. "Show her, Obsidian."

The battle-droid extended its hand, revealing the small silver device. Smooth-sided and circular, it looked innocuous enough; although, at the sight of it, bile stung the back of Aria's throat.

"We need to destroy it," Vic said, snapping the container closed. "Or your friends will locate us the moment we come out of hyperspace."

"Do it then," she murmured, wrapping her arms about her torso. It was cool inside the cabin, yet her discovery made her feel shivery, as if she were coming down with something.

Vic nodded to his first mate, and Obsidian clenched its metal fist, grinding its long fingers together. And when the battle-droid opened its hand once more, only silver dust remained in its palm.

Aria exhaled sharply. She shifted her attention back to Vic, her gaze resting upon his face. "Thank you … again."

His mouth twitched. "No need … I had to destroy that tracker for my own good as well as yours. I'm getting tired of meeting Mir-Ferrin battle-droids everywhere I go." He paused then, picking up the kit and rising to his feet. "And I don't want them following us to Staturine II."

"How's the fish?"

Aria glanced up from where she had been picking at the delicately poached fillet on her plate. Vic sat opposite her at the table. He'd almost cleared his plate, while she was only halfway through hers. Meeting his eye, she forced a smile. "It's not bad … for a synth dish."

Vic picked up a glass of water and took a sip. His gaze then dropped to where she continued to push the fish around with her fork. "If there's nothing wrong with the meal, your appetite must be off."

Aria sighed and laid down her fork. "It is." She pulled a face then. "Can you blame me?"

"No," he replied, using a scrap of bread to mop up the last of the buttery sauce on his plate. "But if you aren't going to eat that, I will."

Aria nodded, pushing the dish across to him.

Vic put his empty plate aside and started on hers. Watching him eat with calm focus, Aria's curiosity got the better of her. "Don't you ever get lonely, Vic?"

He glanced up before shaking his head. "I've got Obsidian for company."

"I know … but you never remain long enough in one place to form connections or put down roots."

"I don't need to do either of those things," he replied, his tone cooling. "That's why I prefer shipping merch to passengers. Machinery parts don't pry."

Ignoring the jibe, Aria leaned forward, her gaze never leaving his face. "But don't you get tired of drifting around the sector, dealing with deadbeats you can never trust?"

Vic snorted. "Firstly, I don't 'drift' around the sector. I ship goods along the major trade routes. And secondly, dealing with backstabbing assholes is part of what makes the job so rewarding … the risk ensures I never lose my edge. Or so I thought."

Aria huffed a laugh, leaning back in her seat and folding her arms across her chest. "I've never met anyone like you before," she murmured. "You're an enigma … a man full of contradictions."

He shrugged and resumed eating.

"You pretend otherwise," Aria continued. "And yet, I suspect you're a good man."

His eye glinted as he swallowed his mouthful. "Why? Because I came to your rescue?"

"Not everyone would have." Aria picked up her glass of water, curving her fingers around its smooth surface. However, she didn't take a sip. "You didn't hesitate either. You're straight-talking, honest."

"And yet I deal in stolen goods." His tone was wry.

"You do … but that's not *who* you are."

"No offense, Aria, but you don't know anything about me." Vic hadn't quite finished her plate, but he pushed it aside now. His face was as expressionless as ever, yet she caught the warning in his voice.

Pulse quickening, Aria held his eye. "I know enough," she said quietly. "You wouldn't plant a bug on someone you cared about without their permission … would you?"

Silence followed her question, and Vic's eye narrowed before he finally replied gruffly, "No."

"And would you hunt down a woman who didn't want to marry you … or set killer-bacteria loose?"

"No."

"See … that already makes you a vastly better man than either my father or my fiancé."

Vic leaned back in his seat and regarded her with a veiled gaze. Meanwhile, Aria's grip tightened on her glass. Another pause stretched out between them before Vic eventually spoke. "You were in trouble, Aria … I *had* to help you. I don't think it makes me noble, but I'll admit I'd like to put a laser bolt through your fiancé's forehead." Their gazes fused before his voice lowered. "You deserve much better."

Tension rippled between them, and suddenly Aria's mouth turned dry. Raising the glass to her lips, she took a gulp of water. "We haven't known each other long, yet you look out for me," she murmured as her pulse quickened. "I can't figure you out, Vic … but I want to."

Vic shook his head and slid out of the booth. "Don't bother," he replied tersely. "You'd only be disappointed."

Rising to his feet, he swiped up their dirty plates, making it clear their conversation was at an end.

This time, Aria heeded the warning while he dumped the plates into the recycler and slammed the chute shut. "We've still got fifteen hours until Staturine II," he announced, his tone still clipped. "We should all get some rest." He turned to where the battle-droid was checking the instrument panel in the cockpit. "Plug yourself in, Obsidian, and shut down for a few hours … I'll take care of things."

Vic moved over to a panel and dimmed the lights. He then glanced at Aria. "I usually keep the temperature cool in here," he said, his manner all business now. "Obsidian prefers it, and my body runs hotter ever since I was transitioned. However, you probably find it too cold. Shall I turn the heating up?"

Aria nodded. She hadn't liked to tell him it was a fridge in here, as she'd already put him out repeatedly—but she didn't have any sleepwear with her, and if he didn't increase the thermostat, she'd have to sleep fully clothed.

Vic turned back to the panel and tapped something. An instant later, warm air filtered into the cabin.

"You know where the bathroom is," he said, gesturing to the door that led into the passageway. "I'll let you use it first."

Aria nodded and pushed herself out of the booth. An awkward quiet fell as she picked up her backpack. When they'd sat down to eat, she hadn't intended to grill the man about his life, yet she had. Recent events had forged a bond between the two strangers—but Vic wasn't comfortable talking about himself.

She'd pushed him too hard, and now things would be strained between them.

Heading toward the passageway door, Aria vowed to let him be for the rest of their journey to Staturine II.

Yes, he fascinated her—but it was best she left it there. She'd already crashed into his life; she shouldn't intrude any further.

The door whispered open, and she stepped out into the narrow passageway. The bathroom was halfway along it, to the left: a cramped, utilitarian cubicle.

Hanging up her bag on the door, Aria dug around for her toothbrush. Then, turning to the mirror, she stared back at her reflection. The strain of the past week was showing. Her face looked hunted, and a nerve flickered under one eye.

Reaching behind her, Aria lifted the hem of her top, her fingertips sliding over the plasti-skin Vic had applied. It no longer throbbed, although the spot would likely be a bit tender for the next couple of days.

She paused then, recalling the brush of his fingers on her naked skin, the firm press of his palm on her lower back. The contact had turned her breathing shallow, had made her momentarily forget he'd been about to extract a tracking device from her back.

Jaw firming, she turned back to the mirror, scowling at her reflection.

*Stop it.*

She was a wanted woman—yet here she was, lusting after her rescuer.

She needed to get a grip. Clearly, she was exhausted and losing her wits.

A few hours of sleep should remedy that.

Returning to the cabin, she let Vic retreat to the bathroom.

In the meantime, she ventured forward to where Obsidian had plugged itself into a socket underneath the console to recharge.

Her gaze lingered on the battle-droid, wondering at the adventures the cyborg and droid had been through over the past years.

"What's it like, traveling with Vic?" she asked, articulating her thoughts without meaning to.

The battle-droid's chin kicked up, and it turned to her, its gaze fastening on her.

Aria stared back, feeling a bit foolish. Of course, she didn't expect Obsidian to answer. The question wasn't one that a droid would even understand.

"It is a good life," the battle-droid rumbled.

Aria stiffened, surprise fluttering through her. "You enjoy it?"

"I do."

"Why?"

The battle-droid inclined its head, considering her question. "I have my liberty … and I have explored from one edge of this sector to the other."

Aria was momentarily rendered speechless. No droid, even the latest model utility-droids, could express themselves so eloquently.

"Is there a place you've visited that you would like to return to?" she asked finally, curious now.

"I prefer planets to space stations," Obsidian replied, gaze still fixed upon her. "Staturine II is the one I enjoy returning to the most … it's pleasantly cool. The hot, dusty planets aren't good for my joints."

"Well, you'll be back there soon enough." Aria moved across to the bunks. "I'll let you recharge … I'm going to get some rest too."

Obsidian nodded. "Sleep well."

Aria smiled. "Thank you, I intend to."

# 11. RISK

VIC LAY ON his back, listening to the gentle hum of the life-support.

Damn it, he couldn't sleep.

Usually, he didn't have any problem drifting off, but now, every time he closed his eyes and waited for sleep to roll over him, all he could hear was Aria's soft voice echoing through his head.

*Don't you ever get lonely?*

Her words were torture. He'd told her he didn't, but it was a lie. If there was a sensation he knew intimately, it was loneliness. Ever since his transitioning, the emptiness inside him had become so vast it echoed. He'd gotten used to it over the years, had even learned to ignore it. But the sensation was always there.

She was right about the other stuff too. Life seemed to be getting on top of him of late.

*I can't figure you out, Vic ... but I want to.*

Those words had made his chest, and another part of his anatomy, ache. He hadn't known Aria Mir-Straken long, but already she'd managed to get under his skin. After she'd said that, he'd wanted to reach across the table and haul her against him, to slant his mouth across hers, to sweep her full lips apart with his tongue and kiss her senseless.

Instead, he'd retreated.

The woman had no idea how sultry she was. Her frankness, delivered with a gentle tone and level gaze, was the sexiest thing he'd ever encountered. She'd been through much in the past days and was understandably upset about the tracking device her father had likely planted, yet her focus earlier had been entirely on him.

She seemed fascinated by him—something Vic wasn't used to these days—and he was still reeling from it.

The bunk above him creaked as Aria shifted position.

He imagined her lying there, clad in nothing but a silky tank top and panties.

Yes, although he'd pretended to ignore her when he'd returned from using the bathroom, he'd noticed what she'd worn to bed. She'd been partially uncovered, one shapely leg bent as she peered at her tablet.

Vic couldn't help it—he imagined those long legs wrapped around his hips as he took her—and his groin started to ache.

*Shit. Don't go there, man.* He clenched his jaw, rolling onto his side and glaring out at the shadowy cabin.

He needed to get to Staturine II and rid himself of his passenger before he did something stupid, something reckless.

Aria's body cried out for sleep, yet her mind wouldn't rest.

She lay awhile on the top bunk, staring up at the ceiling of the cabin and waiting for exhaustion to claim her.

But it didn't.

Earlier, she'd been focused on Vic, yet now that she'd decided to leave the man alone, her focus returned to the bug he'd extracted from her back.

Who had put it there?

Aria drew in a deep breath. *I need to contact father.*

She couldn't call him yet, not while they were in hyperspace. She'd have to wait until they reached Staturine II to do so. Her pulse quickened then; it wasn't a conversation she was looking forward to, for if her suspicions were correct, she wasn't sure what she'd do, or how she'd respond.

She'd had her difficulties with her father over the years—after her mother had died, he'd become even more distant and distracted—but she never thought he'd resort to treating her like his property.

She really thought he had more respect for her than that.

Movement on the bunk below her drew Aria out of her brooding. Eyes flickering open, she rolled over onto her side to see Vic rise to his feet. The dim cabin lights outlined his torso. He wore nothing but loose, drawstring pants that sat low on his hips.

Awareness prickled her skin as her gaze trailed down the long length of his back. The man's body was sculpted muscle.

Barefoot, Vic padded across the cabin and disappeared into the passageway, presumably to use the bathroom.

Aria watched him go, warmth pooling in her lower belly.

Huffing a sigh, she rolled onto her back once more before muttering a curse under her breath.

Wis forgive her, she wasn't used to this strange restlessness. In the past, she'd been too focused on her work to be distracted by sexual attraction.

And then there was Elijah. She had eyes—she knew her fiancé was strikingly attractive—but she still saw him as the older boy she'd befriended as a child.

He'd never set her pulse racing.

But Vic did. Their conversation earlier had made her back off, yet it didn't erase her interest in him.

She was still lying there, wishing her racing thoughts would settle so she could get some rest, when the door slid open, and Vic returned to the cabin.

He stopped at the water dispenser and poured himself a glass. Aria noted that a faint sheen of sweat covered his torso.

"Is it too hot for you in here?" she murmured.

Vic glanced her way, his tall, well-built body tensing. "A little … but I'm okay … did I wake you?"

"No, I couldn't sleep."

He took a gulp of water. "You neither?"

Aria sat up on the bunk, pushed aside the covers, and hung her legs over the side. She'd gone to bed in a tank top and her underwear. The temperature in here was perfect for her, and she enjoyed the warmth feathering over her naked legs. Nonetheless, the air was drying. "Can you pass me a glass of water, please?" she asked.

Vic nodded, finishing his glass, and filling a fresh one for her.

He approached Aria and handed her the water.

Their fingers brushed as she took the glass, and awareness tingled down her arm.

"I'm sorry about earlier," she said softly, trying to ignore the nervous fluttering under her ribcage. "I made assumptions about you … and I shouldn't have."

He shrugged. "Don't apologize. I'm just not used to others showing any interest in me these days. Most people don't look past my eye plant."

"So, I haven't offended you?"

He shook his head. "If anything … I should be saying sorry to you. I was rude."

She smiled. "I'd prefer to call it 'abrupt'."

He huffed a laugh. Their gazes met then, and his mouth twitched. "You're good company, Aria. I'm just not much of a conversationalist." He then glanced toward the cockpit at the shadowed outline of the battle-droid recharging. "Maybe you're right about me … I spend too much time with Obsidian."

"I had a chat with him earlier," she replied, her smile widening. "It was surprising."

His gaze flicked back to her. "How so?"

"Obsidian loves traveling around the sector with you … discovering new worlds, experiencing new things."

"And why does that surprise you?"

Aria lifted her glass to her lips and drained it in a few gulps. "I didn't think droids … least of all battle-droids … were built to experience likes or dislikes."

She handed the glass back to Vic, who dropped it into the recycler.

"Battle-droids aren't," he replied, turning back to her. "But when I had him reprogrammed on Goarthin … I requested a few special mods."

Aria inclined her head. Goarthin was just one system away from her home planet. "A Mir-Straken technician worked on him?"

"Only the best."

Aria studied his face, wishing she could read him easier. "So, you really do enjoy this life, Vic?"

He nodded. "Far more than I liked my previous one, at least." He paused then, moving back toward the bunks. He halted before her, his chin lifting to hold her gaze. "It has its moments ... but I was never my own master before."

Aria considered his words. "You know ... I always thought I was in control of my own destiny ... but I don't think I was," she admitted finally. "I'm beginning to realize I've been living up to other people's expectations of me. Maybe a life of freedom ... like yours ... would suit me, after all."

Vic folded his arms across his bare chest, leaning up against the ladder to the top bunk. "You know your own mind, Aria. I'm surprised a woman like you would agree to an arranged marriage."

She pulled a face. "I kind of fell into it. Agreeing to marry Elijah was just ... easy."

"Easy?"

Aria sighed. "That sounds bad, doesn't it? I suppose I've spent too long focusing on my work ... hardly bothering to glance up and look around me."

"Your research means a lot to you?"

"It does." Aria paused then, noting the discomfort that tightened her chest. She wasn't used to examining her own decisions so closely. "But the past days have made me question that too. At first, I threw myself into my work to prove something to my father, but these days, I'm beginning to wonder if I've been using it as an escape."

Vic's gaze held hers. "What are you escaping?"

Her breathing grew shallow. "I don't know ... uncertainty maybe ... risk." She stopped then, embarrassment warming her cheeks. Gods, she was letting her mouth run away with her today. She wanted to look away but found she was unable to.

Vic didn't reply immediately. Instead, he reached up and placed his hand over where hers curled around the edge of the mattress.

Aria caught her breath, and a weighty silence settled over the cabin.

"We're all running away from something," Vic murmured finally.

Aria swallowed, to ease the sudden tightness in her throat. The huskiness of his voice whispered over her skin. "And what have you been running from, Vic Mir-Riorde?"

He lifted his hand from hers and traced her wrist with his fingertip. Aria shivered at the gentleness of his touch. "This," he whispered.

Aria exhaled slowly. Her heart was beating fast now, and she was starting to feel a little light-headed. Suddenly, it felt overly hot inside this cabin.

Wordlessly, she slid down from her bunk, landing lightly on the floor. She then stepped closer to him and raised her chin to hold his gaze.

Vic didn't move. Instead, he swallowed, his throat bobbing.

Inhaling deeply, Aria raised her right hand, placing it upon his chest, over his heart. A black metal plate, like the one fixed into his right eye socket, covered his right pectoral muscle. However, she wasn't focused on that; instead, she was paying attention to the way his heart pounded against her palm.

Cyborgs were supposed to have a slower pulse than humans, but Vic's heart was racing, just as hers was.

A moment later, his hand covered hers. He cleared his throat then. "Aria ... I—"

"Kiss me, Vic."

He lifted a hand, sliding his knuckles along the line of her jaw before he cupped the back of her neck and drew her to him.

His lips brushed against hers, softly at first, and then increasing in pressure—and when his tongue slid into her mouth, Aria melted against him.

# 12. HARD TO RESIST

THE KISS WAS gentle, sensual, and thorough—it robbed Aria of breath and made her senses reel. Dizziness swept over her, a soft moan rising from her throat.

Vic grazed her bottom lip with his teeth, pulling Aria a little closer, before he kissed her again, deeper this time.

She whimpered. He tasted good. The rasp of his stubble against the smooth skin of her cheek caused hunger to knot inside her.

A restless, pulsing ache started between her thighs, and she leaned into him, craving more.

When Vic eventually drew back from the kiss, they were both breathing hard.

Aria gazed into his face, held by the intensity of his single eye. "Do that again," she whispered, thrilling at her own boldness.

Vic let out a low, shuddering sigh and stepped into her once more, pulling her into his arms. His mouth then savaged hers.

Aria's arms slid up his chest, linking around his neck, as she kissed him back with equal passion. Their tongues dueled, tangled, and Aria forgot where they were. Her body had a will of its own now.

Vic ripped his mouth from hers then, his lips trailing down her jaw to her throat. The tip of his tongue traced a path down the column of her neck to the hollow between her collarbones.

Reaching up, he grasped the wrist of her hand that still splayed across his chest and guided it down, moving her palm over his groin and gently pressing it against him.

Aria caught her breath. The feel of a hot, hard erection—tenting the thin material of his pants, and pressing against her palm—made excitement quicken in her veins.

Heart kicking against her breastbone, Aria slid her hand down the long length of him. She was about to repeat the action when Vic's grip on her wrist tightened, stilling her.

An instant later, he growled a curse and took hold of the hem of her tank top, pushing it up.

Aria helped him, wriggling out of the garment and tossing it onto the floor.

Vic's lips parted, his chest heaving as he stared down at her breasts. Following his gaze, Aria saw that they jutted shamelessly toward him, her swollen nipples a deep dusky-brown in the dim light.

With another whispered oath, he scooped her breasts up in his hands, holding them high. He then bent his head and devoured one of them.

Aria cried out as he sucked hard on her nipple, drawing it deep into his hot mouth.

The aching pulse between her thighs grew intense now, and she writhed against him.

There was something about this man that drove her wild—an intoxicating blend of strength, sensuality, and vulnerability that she found hard to resist.

Vic shifted his attention to her other breast, and with each suck, warm, rippling pleasure arrowed through her loins.

By the time he drew back, she was gasping for breath, her legs trembling.

Vic stared down at her, and Aria saw the hunger burning in his eye.

Whispering her name, he reached down and hooked his fingers over the waistline of her panties before pulling them down. Sheer black satin slid down her legs, and Aria kicked them aside.

Vic didn't waste any time after that—pushing her back against the ladder that led up to the top bunk, he spread her wide. His fingertips traced a sensual path down over the curve of her belly, to the soft chestnut curls between her thighs.

And when his fingers touched her there, she inhaled sharply.

He slid her up the ladder, holding her up easily while he placed a foot on one of the rungs so she could brace herself against his body.

The position left her fully exposed to him, making the desire knotting in her lower belly tighten. She felt freed, powerful, and her breathing quickened further when his gaze raked down her heaving breasts, over her belly, to between her spread thighs.

"Beautiful," he whispered, stroking her sex with his fingers. And when he began to rub her there, she gasped, delicious warmth flooding through her.

He didn't stop, working her gently with the pad of his thumb. And all the while, he watched her, his chest rising and falling sharply now.

His focus on her was erotic, and it wasn't long before he took her over the edge. Heat pulsed between her spread legs. Tingling started then before pleasure spiked deep through her womb.

Arching against him, Aria cried out. Her head fell back, her eyelids fluttering shut as she rode the waves of her climax.

Vic held her up as she writhed and trembled.

Breathing hard, Aria opened her eyes and curled forward, meeting his gaze once more. She reached out, her hands sliding down his chest, down his flat belly, to the waistband of his pants.

She might not be able to read his face, but his body told another story. She felt him tremble under her fingertips, heard the excited rasp of his breathing—and when she pushed down his pants, the head of his shaft was slick with need.

Her fingers encircled his girth, and she stroked him, marveling at the iron heat of his cock and the way it jerked in her grip.

Sighing his name, she angled his shaft toward her, stroking its tip between her spread, trembling thighs. His hands slid under her, grasping her backside tight as he moved close. He entered her in one slow, smooth thrust—and was halfway in when a stinging pain made Aria catch her breath.

Freezing in his arms, her fingernails biting into his biceps, she dragged in a deep breath.

Vic's chin kicked up, his gaze widening. "Have I hurt you?" he rasped.

"No," she whispered back. "I'm fine." It was true, the pain was fleeting, and an instant later, a languorous, pulsing heat replaced it. "Keep going."

Still holding her eye, he nodded. He then sank into her, sliding to the hilt. And this time, there was no discomfort, only the delicious sensation of being filled, stretched.

Aria groaned, spreading her legs wider still to accommodate him.

Bending his head to her, Vic claimed her mouth once more, kissing her deeply as he rotated his hips, grinding into her.

Pleasure crested once more, and suddenly she was writhing against him. Her fingernails bit into his upper arms again, although not from pain this time. Her body no longer felt her own; sweat trickled down her back and between her breasts.

Vic's hands slid from her backside to her thighs, where he gripped her legs and wrapped them around his hips.

He then took her in slow, deep thrusts, each one pushing her farther up the ladder. Aria let go of his upper arms, clutching at his shoulders instead, while he buried his face in her neck, his teeth nipping the sensitive skin there.

And with each thrust, he touched a place deep inside that made her core turn liquid.

Aria went wild, driving herself down on him.

Vic was pounding into her now, as savage as she was.

She shattered then, her cry echoing through the cabin. She clung desperately to him as if she'd spiral out into the depths of space otherwise, her pulse thundering in her ears.

Vic plunged into her once more, and then he bent his head, muffling his own raw cry in Aria's neck as his sweat-slick body went rigid against hers.

Vic held her there, pinned against the ladder for a while, the pair of them clinging together, panting, until the storm passed.

Since his transitioning, he'd paid for sex in a pleasure house a handful of times. It was the only intimacy he could get these days, yet the experience had been empty, merely a way to satisfy a physical urge.

Even before his transitioning, it had never been like this. Vic had never let go in the past, not like he just had.

Sliding his lips up Aria's throat, feeling the flutter of her pulse there, Vic kissed his way up to her jaw, before his mouth found hers. The kiss was slow and sensual, even while his heart still slammed hard against his breastbone.

He cradled her soft, lush body against him.

"Your back," he murmured finally, concern rising. He'd taken her hard against that ladder, heedless of the cut near her spine. "Is it all right?"

"It's fine," she whispered.

His gaze searched her face. Right from the first, he'd noticed this woman's beauty, but she'd never looked as lovely as she did now. Her green eyes were dark in the dimness, her full lips parted. "You should have told me it was your first time," he said after a pause.

"Why?" she asked softly. "Would you have acted differently, if I had?"

He wasn't sure. "Were you saving yourself for marriage?" he asked then, curious to know why the lovely Aria Mir-Straken was still a virgin at twenty-six.

She huffed a laugh. "I suppose so … this will sound strange, but I never really had much interest in sex." She paused then, her long lashes fluttering against her cheeks as she dropped her gaze, embarrassed now. "I can't believe what I was missing out on."

Vic almost told her that sex wasn't always like that. He'd had enough hollow encounters over the years to know what they'd just experienced together was something special. However, he managed to swallow the comment. He was still reeling, still buried deep inside her. He'd likely say something he'd regret later.

Taking hold of Aria's hips, he withdrew from her in a slow drag that caused a rush of warm seed to spill from her and run down her thighs. Aria gave a groan of disappointment, but he lowered her to the ground and stepped away.

He retrieved some tissues from the locker beside the bunks and handed her some. "Here."

They cleaned themselves up, and Vic pulled up the loose drawstring pants he slept in.

His attention then returned to Aria. Still gloriously naked, she leaned against the ladder as she wiped between her legs.

Watching her, Vic's pulse quickened once more, his cock stirring in his pants.

*Down, boy.* Fucking Aria once had untethered him; twice would make him do and say rash things he'd want to take back later.

He needed time to recover, to pull himself together.

Even so, he didn't want this to be over just yet. Approaching Aria once more, he took the tissues from her and threw them into the trash compactor. He then slid onto his bunk, drawing her with him, and pulling a blanket over them. "We both need to get some sleep," he murmured.

Aria yawned. "You're right … I'm exhausted." She stretched out against his left side. The bed was narrow, which meant they'd be sleeping close. Her body molded against his, and she placed her cheek on his chest, one delicately boned hand spanning his breastbone. Her fingertips brushed the metal plate upon his right pectoral, and Vic fought the urge to wince.

He'd been relieved she hadn't touched his eye plant or chest plate while they'd been having sex; he didn't want to be reminded that he was part machine.

Aria's fingers moved upward then, fastening around the dog tags he wore around his neck. Turning them over, she lifted her head to peer at the details written on them. His name, clan, ID, and blood type. "Why do you still wear these?" she asked softly.

Vic's hand closed over hers. "It's the only link I have to my past," he murmured. "After my transitioning, I was afraid I'd forget who I was. When I woke up in hospital, the dog tags were in a tray next to the bed. They usually throw them away; cyborgs are fitted with an ID chip in the arm and lose their old identity … but I took mine."

Her gaze met his. "Do you still have your ID chip too?"

"No, I cut it out."

"And you've never forgotten who you are?"

"No."

Aria lowered her cheek to his chest once more, and he felt her relax against him.

It had been a long while since he'd lain like this with a lover. Pleasure house workers charged extra for cuddling, but even before that, the moments of intimacy had been few and far between: a marine's life wasn't conducive to relationships.

Silence settled over the cabin then, the only sounds the low hum of the life-support, the whoosh of heating, and the occasional soft beep from the cockpit as Obsidian continued to recharge.

Aria sank against him, her breathing slowing and deepening as she fell asleep.

Cradling her in his arms, Vic continued to stare up at the bottom of the top bunk.

# 13. PERMISSION GRANTED

ELIJAH MIR-FERRIN LEANED back in his seat and frowned. "Are you sure you've lost them?"

The figure projected on the holo-screen before him, a man dressed in black and bronze body armor, dipped his head. "The signal has vanished, My Lord."

"And where were they headed before that, Commander Grav?"

"We have no idea … the tracking sensor doesn't emit a signal while it's in hyperspace … but it's been twenty hours, and they haven't resurfaced," the commander replied, his long face somber. Behind Grav stood two battle-droids. Elijah had sent a squad of them, led by his most trusted commander, after his fiancée. He'd expected them to have caught Aria by now, but she still eluded them.

"You must have an idea of where they went?" Elijah asked after a pause. "Which are the most popular destinations from Calberic?"

"Calberic is close to Mir-Brennan territory, My Lord." The commander shifted his weight awkwardly. "They may have gone there."

Silence fell while Elijah digested this news. The humiliation of being jilted still stung. Why had Aria run? They were supposed to be friends. They respected each other, and yet she'd given her life up—her career and a marriage that would strengthen the alliance between their clans—to become a fugitive.

He didn't understand her behavior at all.

On the other side of the wide marble desk between them, his brother Lucas reclined on a high-backed chair, his expression veiled. After a pause, he spoke up. "Frankly, commander, I'm surprised Aria has managed to avoid you."

"It appears she found an ally on Lanthor," Commander Grav replied. "She's been traveling on a D-Class freighter, *The Wayfarer*, ever since."

Elijah inclined his head. "D-Class … it's one of ours?"

"Yes, My Lord. It's captained by Vic Mir-Riorde, a trader." The commander paused there, his own brow furrowing. "I did some digging … and discovered he's also one of ours. A cyborg turned rogue. He deserted six years ago." The distaste in Grav's voice was evident.

"Why would a cyborg be helping Aria?" Elijah hadn't heard of any cases of rogue cyborgs; the transitioning process robbed them of free will. But clearly, something hadn't worked out with this one if he was captaining a freighter.

"I don't know, My Lord."

"She's probably paying him," Lucas drawled. "Aria's clever enough to know she can't evade capture on her own."

His brother had a point. However, Elijah kept his focus on Grav. "Thank you for the update, Commander. Set a course for the nearest Mir-Brennan system and begin your search there." He paused then, forcing back a grimace. "I don't think you'll have much luck finding my fiancé if she no longer has a tracking device on her. However, you might as well keep looking for a while longer."

The commander gave a brisk nod. "Yes, My Lord. I will update you on our progress in twenty-four hours, as usual."

Elijah nodded before leaning forward and pressing a button on the console before him, cutting the call.

The holo-image vanished.

Rising from his desk, Elijah strode to the broad, floor-to-ceiling window that curved around the circular solar, and stared out at the glowing surface of Formidian—the planet this space station orbited.

"Heartbroken?"

Elijah glanced over his shoulder to see Lucas smirking.

"No," he replied smoothly, "But I expected *you* to look more crestfallen. You need Aria's help, after all."

Lucas made an airy gesture with his hand. "I've already given up on your fiancée. If she's changed her mind about you … the woman's never going to help find a cure for the Starellusbacter."

Elijah tensed. "Aria's worth more to me than that, you know?"

Lucas barked a laugh. "Is she? Come on, brother. It's an arranged marriage … you've never even fucked her."

Elijah didn't reply. Instead, he shifted his attention back to the view through the layers of tempered glass. The sight of the topaz planet, lighting up against the void, cleared his mind. Once again, Lucas had a point. He and Aria had never had sex, hadn't even kissed, but they'd been friends. Elijah was attracted to her—she'd grown from a thin, frizzy-haired girl, into a voluptuous beauty—and he'd been looking forward to taking their relationship to the next level.

However, none of that was Lucas's business.

"The Mir-Strakens are important allies," he said after a lengthy pause. "Their technology skills are the best in this sector … we need their expertise … especially now."

Ever since the disaster on Idral a year earlier, things hadn't gone well for the Mir-Ferrins.

The Mir-Brennans were still rebuilding their space-fleet, but in the meantime, they'd restored old alliances with some of the smaller clans. The result had been serious disruption on the sector's major trade routes. Valuable supplies and weapons destined for Platinum 5 had been seized and impounded—and a month earlier, a Mir-Ferrin battleship had been attacked by a flotilla of unidentified ships during a patrol in the Gastira system. The cruiser had sustained considerable damage before managing to make the jump into hyperspace.

Elijah didn't like that the Mir-Brennans had strong allies, while his clan was struggling to hold onto theirs. His father's attack on Idral had made him unpopular, even amongst those who'd once supported him. If the

Mir-Brennans attacked any time soon, the Mir-Ferrins would stand largely alone.

They needed to focus on strengthening their clan's alliances right now. However, Morgan Mir-Straken was fixated on the idea of mingling their bloodlines; he refused to cooperate fully without a marriage alliance.

Damn it, they had to find Aria.

"Do I have your permission to hire another virologist? Aria isn't the only decent one in the sector."

Elijah glanced over at his brother once more. Lucas was smiling, yet there was a familiar glint in his dark eyes. His interest in the deadly bacterium he'd developed was becoming obsessive.

Not for the first time, misgiving feathered down Elijah's spine.

The super-bacteria were safely locked away in a high-security lab here on Platinum 5, but unless a cure for the disease could be found—a proven one—Elijah didn't want it unleashed.

In truth, he wasn't sure he wanted it set free at all.

When Lucas had approached him about recruiting Aria to help find a cure for it, he'd agreed. It made sense to develop antibiotics that could counter something so dangerous. He was also aware that the Mir-Brennans were getting the upper-hand, and something had to be done to redress the balance.

But ever since he'd cleared his brother to continue work on his project, Elijah had been uneasy.

The Mir-Brennans were their enemies, and he wanted to bring them down, wanted vengeance for his father and youngest brother's deaths.

But did he want to take it this way?

Elijah cleared his throat then, pushing aside his worries. "Permission granted," he said gruffly, "but be careful, Lucas. Word can't get out about this."

Lucas grinned back. "Don't worry, it won't."

"I don't think you should make that move, Obsidian."

Seated opposite Aria, the battle-droid shifted his gaze from the board between them, fixing upon her. "And why not?" it queried.

"Because you'll leave your clan-lord vulnerable."

Obsidian inclined his head. "You shouldn't be helping me."

Aria snorted. "Why not … it's clear you haven't played *Clan-lord's Defense* often."

They played upon a carved wooden board. Aria had taken the role of attacker and Obsidian that of defender. The defender had to protect the clan-lord while he moved toward the edge of the board, while the attacker tried to bring him down before he reached it.

"Vic taught me recently," the droid admitted, reaching out a large black hand, grasping hold of the clay figurine, and shifting it sideways. "I'm still learning how to strategize."

"Well, I grew up playing this game with my father," she replied.

Aria's stomach tightened then, mentioning Morgan Mir-Straken reminded her that she'd have to call him soon.

Pushing aside her nervousness, she motioned to the board. "Although we always played with a holo-board … not the real thing."

"I found this in a market on Helix 8," Obsidian replied. "Vic said games like these are good for developing my neuro pathways." The droid then straightened up in his seat. "Your turn."

Aria's gaze swept the board before she sighed. "That move wasn't any better," she replied. Reaching forward, she moved one of her counters, wiping out two of the clan-lord's defending pawns, before she knocked over the clan-lord's figurine. "I win."

Obsidian's gaze dropped to the board, and it made a rumbling sound, one that almost sounded like a growl. "I must practice further," it declared. "Shall we play again?"

"I don't think so." Vic's voice intruded. "We're about to make our final approach … get yourself up here, Obsidian."

The battle-droid quickly packed away the game before rising from the table at the back of the cabin. It then returned to the cockpit in long strides.

Aria got up and joined them, standing behind the pilot and copilot as their destination hove into view.

To their left, a massive Mir-Brennan battleship was orbiting Staturine II.

Vic hit a button on the console in front of him.

"*Star Tempest*, this is *The Wayfarer* … permission requested to enter Staturine II airspace and to land at Castle Valnor."

A pause followed before a comms-officer onboard the battleship replied, "Welcome back, *Wayfarer*. Copy, you're cleared."

Vic clicked off the comm channel and started to adjust the controls.

"That was friendly," Aria murmured.

"I'm on good terms with the Mir-Brennans," he replied.

"But you're flying a Mir-Ferrin freighter … surely, that makes them nervous?"

"Usually, it would, but *The Wayfarer* has special status." He glanced over his shoulder then, meeting her eye. "Go on … you'd better strap yourself in."

Aria returned to the cabin, sank down into a seat at the end of the row, and clipped on her harness. She sighed, enjoying the sense of well-being that suffused her. She'd woken up earlier relaxed and clear-headed. Despite that she'd been reluctant to wash the scent of Vic off her skin, she'd taken a hot shower and dressed.

Over the past couple of hours, Vic had been busy—and a little distracted. But every time their gazes met, and held, warmth flowed over her. It was difficult not to reach for him, not to seek out his mouth with hers.

Pushing aside heated, sexy thoughts, Aria shifted her attention to Staturine II. The planet's curve drew closer. Streamers of cloud and mottled patches of green, brown, and blue covered its surface.

The freighter shuddered as it entered the atmosphere, the engines changing pitch to compensate.

They were heading toward the planet's southern capital, Briscay. Staturine II was a mining planet, one of the richest in the sector. The Mir-Brennan clan had originated here, although they'd spread out far and wide over the past millennia, populating many of the surrounding systems.

Aria had never visited this planet, for her clan had little to do with the Mir-Brennans. Nonetheless, she'd heard of Staturine II's mines, and the wealth of minerals—which were used largely in medicines—it produced. The planet sat on the edge of Mir-Brennan territory, close to the Mir-Leliths, and the two clans had been in dispute for centuries over the planet's mining rights.

More recently, they'd been at war, after the Mir-Lelith ambassador had tried to assassinate the Mir-Brennan clan-lord. However, over the last year, they'd managed to negotiate a ceasefire—and if the newsfeeds were to be believed, they were in discussions about sharing Staturine II's riches once more.

*The Wayfarer* nosed its way down and then leveled out, skimming across a glittering sea before they crossed onto a mountainous continent. Even from up here, Aria could see the planet was a cold one. Snow capped most of the mountains, even the low ones, and forests of dark conifers carpeted the valleys and plains below. Grey rock studded the landscape, and Aria made out huge craters—the open-cast mines that pock-marked the planet's surface. A network of shunt rails traced the rocky terrain, ferrying ore between the mines and the storage depots.

When Briscay hove into sight, Aria wasn't surprised to note that many of the buildings were made of the same grey rock as the surrounding landscape. Even so, it was beautiful. A towering citadel of slender spires, Briscay sparkled in the sun, and at its heart rose a great dove-grey fortress: Castle Valnor. Turreted towers pierced the sky, and from one of them, the gold and black Mir-Brennan flag rippled in the breeze—a signal that the clan-lady was in residence.

"Where are we landing?" Aria called out.

"The castle has its own docking station," Vic replied as he brought the freighter around in a loop. "We're heading there."

"Really? You don't need special clearance for that?"

Vic glanced over his shoulder then, their gazes meeting for an instant. "I *have* special clearance."

Aria cocked her head. The ease with which he'd entered Staturine II airspace, and his clearance to land by the clan-lady's front door, made her realize there was something he wasn't telling her. Fighting the urge to question him, she watched as they circled the castle, lowering while Vic prepared to make his approach to the landing bay.

Craning her neck forward, Aria took in the spiderweb of streets below, where sleek hoppers sped in amongst shunts that ferried passengers from one side of the city to the other.

At the base of the sheer castle walls, a great maw yawned open to admit them. Vic guided *The Wayfarer* inside, bringing the freighter to a shuddering halt amongst a line of gleaming gilded shuttles.

Vic murmured something to Obsidian and pushed himself up out of his seat. He then entered the cabin and reached for his utility vest, pulling it on.

Aria rose to her feet, grabbed her backpack, and slung it over her shoulder. She then flashed Vic an arch look. "I suppose you're going to tell me we don't have to request an audience with the clan-lady?"

He turned to her, his mouth twitching. "That's right. Lady Jenna will be waiting for us."

# 14. FOREWARNED IS FOREARMED

ARIA FOLLOWED VIC down the ramp, adjusting her cloak as she went. Her clothing, although practical, wasn't the right attire to meet the leader of the Mir-Brennan clan in, but she didn't have anything else.

Vic hadn't bothered to change either.

"So." Aria cleared her throat, curiosity finally getting the best of her. "Is there a reason why you haven't told me you're friends with Jenna Mir-Brennan?"

Vic glanced over his shoulder. "It never came up," he replied with a shrug. "I would have told you if it had … it's no secret."

Aria arched an eyebrow. "Really?" She lengthened her stride to keep up with him as he headed toward the landing bay doors. Two figures, clad in gleaming jet armor, black cloaks hanging from their shoulders, awaited them there. "Out with it then."

Vic slowed so she drew level with him. "A year ago, Lady Jenna hired me and Obsidian to help her rescue her brother, and his wife and daughter. She was on the run with her bodyguard after the Mir-Ferrins seized control of Idral … and her husband sent assassins after her while she was on a diplomatic mission."

Aria's brow furrowed. Like most citizens of the Rith sector, she'd watched the newsreels. Lady Jenna, who'd been the Mir-Brennan ambassador at the time, had gone to negotiate a ceasefire with the Mir-Leliths. In her absence, the Mir-Ferrin space fleet had launched an attack on Mir-Brennan Tower before storming it and taking the clan-lord and his family prisoner. Cathal Mir-Brennan had been scheduled for execution on the day rescuers had freed him.

His sister and her bodyguard had hired mercenaries to help them.

However, the clan-lord hadn't survived the escape attempt. Rumor was that it was Cathal himself who had set off a detonator inside the fortress, sacrificing his own life to kill his enemies. Lady Jenna had managed to get his wife and daughter out though, and now she ruled their clan.

"So, the mercenaries Lady Jenna hired … were you and Obsidian?"

Vic's mouth twitched. "That's right."

A smile curved Aria's lips then. "No wonder she throws open her doors to you."

"Greetings, Captain." One of the black-armored guards greeted Vic as they approached. The guard then nodded to Aria before his gloved hand indicated to the door behind him, where the Mir-Brennan clan insignia—a shooting star above a clenched fist—was emblazoned. "The clan-lady awaits."

Lady Jenna Mir-Brennan rose from the long sofa and flashed Vic a wide smile.

Entering the solar a few steps behind her companion, for she'd deliberately hung back to let Vic go first, Aria noted the pleasure glinting in Lady Jenna's mahogany-hued eyes. She was clearly delighted by his visit.

"Good to see you, Vic." A dark-haired man, who'd been sitting next to Lady Jenna, also got up. They stood in a circular chamber with high ceilings and wide windows overlooking a balcony. Silvery sunlight filtered into the solar.

"And you, Malik," Vic replied, warmth in his voice.

The man's mouth quirked. "Can't keep away, eh?"

Aria viewed the man with interest. *This must be Malik Mir-Draven.*

She'd heard about the clan-lady's consort, and previously her bodyguard. Tall and broad-shouldered, with tanned skin and violet eyes, Malik was a strikingly handsome man. Lady Jenna was clad in a floor-length golden tunic, while her new husband wore a shirt and tight pants of the same color.

Vic shrugged. "It seems not."

"Had a change of heart about accepting the Captain of the Lady's Watch position?" Malik inclined his head. "It's still yours, if you want it?"

Vic's soft snort gave his answer. Aria eyed him with interest. She wasn't surprised he'd turn down such an opportunity. The position was an honor, indeed, but Vic valued his freedom.

"Don't harass the man," Lady Jenna chided her husband softly. She then approached Vic, smiling once more. "You're always welcome … but something tells me this isn't a social call." Her gaze flicked to Aria, curiosity lighting in those soulful brown eyes. "Are you going to introduce us to your friend?"

Aria stepped forward and extended her hand before Vic had the chance to answer. "Aria Mir-Straken … pleased to meet you, My Lady."

Lady Jenna inclined her head, smiling once more. "Mir-Straken … that's not a clan name I hear often in this corner of the sector."

"Aria is the Mir-Straken clan-lord's daughter," Vic replied. "And until a week ago, she was Elijah Mir-Ferrin's fiancée."

The warmth on Lady Jenna's face froze, and Aria cast Vic an exasperated look. She was getting to that—he didn't need to be so blunt.

"I *was* engaged to the Mir-Ferrin clan-lord," she admitted, "but I jilted Elijah on the morning of our wedding and have been on the run ever since."

Behind Lady Jenna, Malik drew close, his dark brows knitted together.

"Vic saved me from my pursuers on Lanthor … and he's helped me elude capture a couple of times now … but that's not why he brought me here." Aria halted then, drawing in a deep breath. "I have something important to tell you."

Jenna Mir-Brennan's face grew increasingly grave the further Aria got into her story. They'd all taken a seat on the sofas, which formed a square in the center of the polished stone floor. The clan-lady and her consort sat facing Aria and Vic.

Aria hated being the bearer of ill-tidings, but the Mir-Brennans had to be warned.

When she finished her tale, a heavy silence fell in the solar.

Eventually, Jenna rose to her feet and stalked to the windows, staring out at the encircling, snow-capped mountains. When she spoke, her voice was tight. "Do they know what they're risking?"

"Yes," Aria replied. "But Lucas is obsessed with this project, and Elijah is desperate to claw back Mir-Ferrin control in this sector. He's not thinking straight."

Malik snorted. "So, he's agreed to let his brother create a super-bacterium to wipe the rest of us out?"

"Everyone needs a hobby," Vic quipped.

Jenna cursed then, her shoulders rigid as she continued to stare out the window, hands clenched at her sides. A moment later, she swiveled, her gaze spearing Aria's.

There was strength on her face, determination. "How easy is it to create medicine to counteract such a bacterium?"

Aria held her gaze. "It isn't … that's why Lucas wanted my assistance."

"Surely, they won't release the bacteria without having a cure for it first," Malik said. He was leaning back, one ankle crossed over the knee. However, despite his apparently relaxed stance, his gaze was sharp. "Elijah Mir-Ferrin isn't an idiot."

Aria's mouth thinned. No, he wasn't. All Mican Mir-Ferrin's sons were sharp-witted, cunning. Nonetheless, she'd always thought Elijah different to his younger brothers, more measured in his reactions and not so blinkered by ambition and greed. How mistaken she'd been.

"You're right about Mir-Ferrin being desperate," Lady Jenna murmured, turning back to the window. "He didn't expect our allies to support us so fiercely, while their own deserted them. Our eyes on the inside inform us there have been several failed talks with their allied clans. It appears many of them didn't sanction Mican Mir-Ferrin's unprovoked attack on Idral."

Aria stilled. It shouldn't have surprised her that the Mir-Brennans would have spies, agents, on Platinum 5. She then wondered how many eyes Elijah had planted on Staturine II. "Congratulations," she murmured. "You've made your enemy nervous."

Jenna glanced over her shoulder, her mouth curving into a humorless smile. "We have … but a cornered serpent is even more dangerous."

Aria realized then, not that she'd doubted it earlier, that this woman was far more than she appeared. Her soft, feminine appearance hid a sharp mind and strong will. It took strength to lead a clan, a responsibility that Aria wouldn't have wanted.

"The Mir-Ferrins know I plan to take Idral back." Lady Jenna went on. "And they'll have learned that we've almost regained our former strength."

"They also want revenge for what Cathal did," Vic pointed out. "Biological warfare could give them the edge they crave."

The clan-lady nodded, her full lips compressing. Folding her arms across her chest, she turned fully from the window, her attention never leaving Aria's face. "I thank you for bringing me this news," she murmured. "Forewarned is forearmed."

# 15. OFF-GUARD

TOWELING OFF HER hair, Aria padded barefoot across the cool, polished stone floor to the large, canopied bed that dominated her bedchamber. She then picked up her tablet and switched it on.

It was less than an hour until she and Vic were expected at dinner with the clan-lady and her family. She had time to make an important, long-overdue call.

Hanging up her towel over the back of a chair, she placed the tablet on the desk by the window and opened an encrypted channel to Haliaen.

Her planet was nearly two thousand light years away, but it took just a few seconds to establish the connection.

Breathing slowly and deeply, Aria leaned the tablet upon a stand and waited, steeling herself to face her father.

Even so, when his image materialized on the screen, her throat thickened, the back of her eyes burning. She'd grown apart from her father over the years, yet he was all she had left.

Morgan Mir-Straken's green eyes fastened upon her, his lips parting. "Aria!" He leaned forward then, his face growing taut. "Where are you?"

Aria stiffened. It wasn't the greeting she'd hoped for, but she shouldn't have expected any different.

"Hello, father," she greeted him, deliberately not answering the question. "As you can see, I'm safe and well."

His brow furrowed. "Clearly." His gaze roamed past her as he tried to make out her surroundings. However, Aria had been careful to place the tablet where he couldn't see the view out of the windows, or anything that would let him know she was with the Mir-Brennans. "But Nain take you, girl ... where have you been?"

"I'm sorry if I've worried you," Aria replied, swallowing. Naming the Goddess of the Dark wasn't to be taken lightly. "But it was too risky to get in contact."

The clan-lord's dark brows knitted together. "You'd better explain yourself," he said, his voice hardening. "I spared no expense on that wedding and invited guests from across the sector. Do you have any idea how humiliating it was when Elijah Mir-Ferrin demanded to know where his bride was? Do you even care about the diplomatic incident you caused?"

Heat ignited in the pit of Aria's belly.

It only took a few moments for her to remember why she and her father weren't close. His focus was on allying the Mir-Strakens to a ruling clan—and she was his tool to do it.

His words reminded her why she'd called him in the first place.

It wasn't to tell him about what the Mir-Ferrins were planning or to assure him she was safe and well.

It was to discover the truth.

Clenching her jaw, she leaned back in her chair and stared her father down. "A few hours ago, I had a tracking device removed from my lower back," she said finally. "Did you have it put there?"

Morgan Mir-Straken's face went still, his gaze widening.

He regained control an instant later, but it was enough. Aria had seen the truth.

She folded her arms across her chest and looked down at him. "Why would you plant a bug on me?"

He scowled. "I didn't."

"It was when my eggs were harvested, wasn't it?"

Her father heaved a sigh. However, under his coppery complexion, he'd paled. She'd caught him off-guard, as she'd intended, in a lie.

"This is ridiculous, Aria," he said after a pause, adopting the same tone he'd used when she'd been a child—the one that told her she was being over-emotional and irritational. "I don't know what you're talking about."

"Don't you? I thought it strange the Mir-Ferrins turned up everywhere I went. You didn't waste any time in telling Elijah I could be tracked, did you?"

The clan-lord's expression hardened. "Enough of this. You still haven't answered my questions. *Why* did you run, and *where* are you now?"

Heat swept through Aria, pulsing in her gut. Unfolding her arms, she leaned forward, her gaze never leaving her father's. There was no concern on his face, just outrage. He wasn't sorry or even embarrassed that she'd caught him out.

Instead, he was twisting their exchange back in his favor. He was trying to establish control, as he always did.

"You won't answer my questions, so I won't answer yours," she replied coldly. "Goodbye, father."

And with that, she cut the call.

Aria's chest ached as she slid into the chair the utility-droid had drawn out for her. Seating herself at the long, gleaming table, she sucked in a deep breath, willing the tightness under her breastbone to subside.

It felt as if her father had just stabbed her between the ribs.

Vic sat down at her side. To her surprise, he'd changed clothing, and was now dressed in a high-necked navy-blue tunic, black leather pants that molded to his muscular form, and high boots. She caught the faint scent of spicy cologne then and noted that his hair was still slightly damp from showering.

They'd been given separate bedchambers, and, despite that she'd wished for privacy when she spoke to her father, Aria had been a little disappointed they wouldn't be sharing the same quarters.

After what had happened between them onboard *The Wayfarer,* she longed to be physically close to him again.

And after speaking with her father, she could have done with a hug.

She hadn't told Vic yet that her father had confirmed her suspicions—that he'd betrayed her. It was all still too raw. If she brought the subject up with him right now, she'd likely go to pieces.

Shoving thoughts of her father to one side—she'd cry into her pillow later—Aria shifted her attention from Vic to the beautifully decorated table and the napkins that had been folded into intricate fans. Such attention to detail.

She lifted her gaze from the table then and focused on the wall opposite—on the floor-to-ceiling mural of Fara. The Goddess of Light held her lantern aloft, against a backdrop of stars. Since her arrival, Aria had learned the people of Briscay—and indeed the southern continent of Staturine II—revered Fara.

Twisting around then, she surveyed the depiction of Fara's sister, Nain, behind her. The Goddess of the Dark, in her cloak of shadows, stood before a black hole, her hands raised to beckon chaos.

It was always the way to have the sisters together— Fara and Nain were opposites, and always at war, but kept balance in the universe.

"Dramatic murals, aren't they?"

Aria turned back to find Lady Jenna smiling at her. She sat at the head of the table, dressed in a shimmering golden halter-neck gown. Her rich brown hair was piled high on her head.

"They are," Aria agreed. The clan-lady's elegance made Aria feel gauche in comparison. Malik sat to Jenna's right, handsome—and more than a little intimidating. "I'd heard the Mir-Brennans were patrons of the arts ... and talented architects ... but I hadn't expected to see such beauty on every corner." It was true, her bedchambers had a breathtaking mural of a space-scape painted along one wall, and sculptures lined most of the hallways she'd traveled along inside Castle Valnor. All the ceilings, including the one inside this dining room, were high and spider-vaulted.

Lady Jenna's smile widened. "This might be a mining planet, but it has some of the most talented artists and architects in the sector."

"Even a rich culture can't make up for a depressing climate though," a woman, seated at the opposite end of the table, quipped. Thin and dark-haired with startling blue eyes, she favored Aria with a thin smile. Next to the woman sat a girl of around six or seven, with similar coloring, who was watching Aria with unabashed curiosity. "It's always cold here," the woman continued. "Even in the height of summer … and the sky is perpetually grey."

Aria glanced over at the single large window at the northern end of the room. Indeed, the sky was overcast.

"We *all* miss the hot, dry climate of Idral," the clan-lady admitted. "Aria … let me introduce you to Isla and Beatrix. My sister-in-law and niece."

Aria smiled before nodding to Isla and her daughter. Of course, Isla was Cathal Mir-Brennan's widow. Dressed in a high-necked black gown that emphasized her slender frame and pale skin, she was striking. However, her gaze was veiled, her pretty face unsmiling.

At the other end of the table, the clan-lady's expression had also sobered. Her gaze rested upon her sister-in-law's face. "One day, we'll walk those streets again, Isla," she murmured. "One day, we'll rebuild Mir-Brennan Tower in Cathal's memory."

Isla's attention shifted to Lady Jenna, her mouth curving into a half-smile, although her expression remained shadowed. "I look forward to that day."

The two women's gazes fused, a silent message passing between them.

The clan-lady then sighed. "There's much to be done," she admitted. "And while we continue our preparations to take back Idral, I've been in drawn-out negotiations with the Mir-Leliths. We've made our peace with them for now, at least, yet they haven't forgotten our promise to share Staturine II's riches with them."

Malik snorted. "Those greedy bastards will never sign a trade agreement."

His wife cast him a quelling look. "They're holding out for equal rights … but that's never going to happen. This planet might lie next to Mir-Lelith territory, but it still belongs to my clan. I must look out for our interests."

Aria listened with interest. Lady Jenna carried the mantle of responsibility well. To rule a galactic clan wasn't easy—as her father had often complained over the years—yet the clan-lady seemed focused on what was best for her people.

Dropping her gaze to the empty plate before her and the neatly laid out cutlery, Aria watched a droid fill her glass with rich Idralian wine. The aroma of roasting meat intruded then as more utility-droids trundled into the dining room, bearing platters of food.

Dinner was served.

They helped themselves to an array of roast meat and spiced vegetables.

Holding up her glass to her dinner companions, Lady Jenna swept her gaze over the table. "To my brother's memory," she announced. "And to our clan returning home … soon." She paused then, her gentle features tightening. "Since stepping into this role, I've worked hard to rebuild our military might. Our weapons experts are currently developing new warheads … missiles that will make pyro-torpedoes seem pitiful in comparison. Next time we meet the Mir-Ferrins in battle, we shall win." Her gaze glinted. "I swear by all the Gods that Idral shall be reclaimed for our people."

"I'll drink to that," Malik murmured, his gaze glinting.

They all raised their glasses.

Taking a sip of the rich red wine, Aria cast a veiled glance in Vic's direction. He met her eye briefly, but as always, she couldn't read him. She wondered what he thought about the Mir-Brennans developing special missiles to use against the Mir-Ferrins.

She supposed she should be thankful it wasn't a bioweapon. Nonetheless, all this talk of war killed her appetite. She lowered her gaze to her plate, spearing a piece of meat with her fork. The food looked delicious, yet her stomach had closed.

Lady Jenna then cleared her throat. "Aria … as I said earlier, I appreciate you telling us about the Starellusbacter."

Aria lowered her fork and glanced up to find the clan-lady watching her.

"However, we can't strike the Mir-Ferrins while they wield such a weapon," the clan-lady went on. "Even if we get our planet back, the victory will be a hollow one if they act rashly. Idral could end up a graveyard."

Both Malik and Isla's expressions turned grave at this, while Aria's pulse quickened. The same thought had occurred to her.

"This bacterium is too dangerous to ignore." Lady Jenna's gaze never left Aria's face. "Someone has to destroy it."

# 16. A CALCULATED RISK

THE SILENCE THAT followed had a weight to it—as if the gravitational pull of the planet had suddenly altered and was dragging them all down toward the floor.

Meanwhile, Jenna Mir-Brennan stared Aria down.

There was no mistaking the steel in the clan-lady's eyes.

The backs of Aria's arms prickled. Eventually, she cleared her throat. "You want me to do it, don't you?"

A sickly sensation swept over her then. Lady Jenna was clever. She wasn't going to ask outright—she wanted Aria to be the one to say it.

The clan-lady nodded, her expression suddenly intent. "Will you?"

"Are you serious, Jenna?" Vic interrupted, his voice roughening. "You can't ask Aria to do this ... it's suicide."

"No, it isn't," Lady Jenna replied, her voice level and firm, while her attention remained upon Aria. "Not, if we plan properly. I have agents on the inside on Platinum 5 ... they'll assist Aria."

Vic swore explosively, earning a quelling look from Isla. Beatrix still sat next to her, wide-eyed now. "Let one of them do it then!"

"None of them are scientists," the clan-lady countered. "The Starellusbacter needs to be handled by someone who knows what they're doing."

"For fuck's sake," Vic growled. "I can't believe you're even suggesting this. I didn't bring Aria here so you could throw her to the Mir-Ferrins."

Aria couldn't believe it either; she felt blind-sided. Taking a large gulp of wine, she let the heat pool in her stomach. Lady Jenna was indeed far tougher, and more ruthless, than she seemed.

"We'll take every precaution we can," the clan-lady replied, not bothered by Vic's response. Of course, she'd been her brother's ambassador for years before she stepped into the role of clan-lady. She knew how to handle difficult situations and aggression.

Next to her, Malik remained silent. However, his big body was tense, his violet eyes narrowed, as he watched Vic. Aria sensed he was readying himself to step in, should Vic forget himself.

Lady Jenna's gaze met Aria's once more. "You'll travel in disguise, and we'll provide you with a fake ID," she said. "We should be able to get you security clearance for the laboratories as well."

"And if she gets caught?" Vic demanded. "You do realize how the Mir-Ferrins treat criminals? The clan-lord will execute her."

Lady Jenna's mouth pursed, a sign he was starting to irritate her. "She won't get caught."

"Easy for you to say … master-minding this whole thing from the safety of Staturine II."

"Vic," Malik rumbled, a sharp edge to his voice. "That's enough."

Aria reached out and put a hand on Vic's arm, squeezing gently. "It's okay," she murmured. "Let me handle this."

She appreciated him defending her, yet his anger wasn't helping.

Focusing on the clan-lady once more, Aria tried to ignore the watery feeling in her bowels. "So, you're saying it's a calculated risk … not a suicide mission?"

"That's right," Lady Jenna replied. "I'll put every resource I have behind this. The Starellusbacter must be destroyed, and you're the right person to do it."

A chill washed over Aria. "No offense, but we've only just met, My Lady. How do you know I'm up to the job?"

Lady Jenna's gaze never wavered. "I'm a good judge of character."

Vic muttered something under his breath, but both women ignored him.

Tension pulsed through the room. Across the table, Bea's blue eyes glistened as she glanced around at the adults. The girl was too young to fully understand what was going on, yet old enough to know it was serious. It wasn't a conversation they should be having in front of her; indeed, Aria was surprised the clan-lady hadn't left it until later.

She realized then that despite her calm manner and steely gaze, Lady Jenna was desperate. The fate of her clan, of billions of souls, hung in the balance. Her request seemed callous—as if she was willing to sacrifice Aria for the greater good, but one life likely seemed a fair exchange for the survival of an entire clan.

Aria's heart started to kick against her ribs then, as her gaze alighted upon the mural of Fara opposite. Light and Dark. The two forces were locked in an eternal struggle, each fighting for dominance.

The Dark was rising now, and it risked destroying them all.

Something had to be done.

Raising her chin, Aria sucked in a deep, steadying breath. "Okay," she whispered. "I'll do it."

"I can't believe you agreed to this." Vic ground out. "You let Jenna pressure you."

Aria turned from the window, her face composed. "No, I didn't. This was my decision, Vic. I could have said no."

They stood in the lounge between their bedchambers in the quarters the clan-lady had given them. High up in Castle Valnor, with a view of the spires of the Temple to Fara, Goddess of Light, the lounge was simply, yet luxuriously, decorated with pale gold furniture, white walls, and a sparkling chandelier of lights hanging overhead.

When they'd arrived earlier, Vic had found himself admiring the opulent lodgings. But right now, it made his skin crawl. It was a reminder that Jenna Mir-Brennan—

the woman he'd respected and considered a friend—
was going to send Aria on a one-way ticket to Platinum
5.

He'd been a bit disconcerted to discover she was
developing new warheads to deal with her enemies.
However, what came directly after this admission had
floored him.

"She guilted you … made it seem as if there's no one
else who could do the job," he shot back, "but that's
bullshit."

Vic knew he was being aggressive, but he'd had
enough. He'd quietly simmered while Aria and the others
discussed her departure for Platinum 5, the method
she'd use to destroy the bacteria, and her options for
escaping the space station afterward. But when the door
had closed behind them in the lounge that sat between
their separate quarters, and they were alone, his self-
control slipped.

Aria's jaw tightened, and her green eyes glinted. "I
don't like this any more than you do … but Jenna's right.
I know how to handle dangerous biomaterials … how to
dispose of them."

"But to send you in alone. It's—"

"Security on Platinum 5 is tight," she cut him off. "The
mission is more likely to be a success if I go on my own."

Vic inhaled sharply, trying and failing to cool his
temper. "You haven't thought any of this through. You
should have told Jenna you'd sleep on it."

Aria put her hands on her hips, her chin lifting. "Why?
To give you the chance to persuade me to say no?"

"At least I give a shit what happens to you. Jenna
doesn't."

Aria stiffened. "I thought you liked the clan-lady?"

Vic folded his arms across his chest. "I do, but I never
thought she'd be so ruthless. You're nothing to her, Aria.
She's using you."

Aria's jaw snapped shut. A brittle silence settled
between them, and when she answered, her voice was
clipped. "Bringing me here was your idea."

"It was … and I'm starting to regret it."

"Can't you see what's at stake?"

"I can," he ground out. "I just don't see why you have to be the one to go on this mission."

"There's no one else."

He snorted. "There's *always* someone else."

Her nostrils flared. "That's the motto you live by, isn't it? If someone isn't handing over hard credits, you aren't interested in helping, are you?"

Heat flushed across his chest. "That's harsh … I saved your ass, didn't I?"

"Yeah, right before you made a detour to Calberic that nearly cost us both our lives."

Vic's pulse quickened. He didn't need reminding of that. Aria was deliberately provoking him, yet her words hit him where it hurt all the same—and maybe he deserved it.

Heaving a deep breath, he approached her, halting when they were just a couple of feet apart. It was dark outside, the view beyond the wide lounge windows revealing an illuminated cityscape and a sea of twinkling lights. The Temple to Fara glowed against the purple-black sky.

"You're right, I look out for myself," he ground out. "You might think that's selfish … but that's why I'm still alive."

# 17. NOT ANYMORE

"THERE'S A PASSENGER liner scheduled to leave at noon for Cadex 12. From there, you can take another flight straight to Platinum 5." Jenna's voice drew Aria out of her brooding. "It's a long trip … but it's the safest way to get from Mir-Brennan to Mir-Ferrin territory."

The two women strolled around a covered walkway that lined one of the castle's many internal courtyards. It was just after breakfast, and wispy clouds covered the pale blue sky. Outdoors, an icy wind no doubt whipped over Briscay, but in here, the temperature was mild.

"I'll make sure I'm on it then," Aria replied.

The clan-lady nodded, although her brow furrowed. "Ever since the attack on Idral, there have been no direct commercial flights between our territories."

"I didn't expect there'd be."

Impatience thrummed through Aria. Four days had passed since she'd made her decision to destroy the Starellusbacter. In that time, she'd spent many hours planning with Jenna and Malik. Her head was now crammed full of details, plans, and warnings.

She was ready to depart, to get underway.

As she'd promised, the clan-lady had thrown herself into assisting Aria however she could. The Mir-Brennans had agents carefully hidden inside Platinum 5. Jenna didn't reveal their names or placements, but within a day, she was able to produce a detailed plan of the space station and the location of the station's virology lab—as well as a list of staff who worked there. Entrance to the laboratory was via keycard and retinal scan.

Aria cast Jenna a side-long glance then, taking in her profile. The clan-lady wore a serious expression this morning, her gaze slightly narrowed as if she was deep in thought. "I can't believe you managed to get me a security pass to the lab," Aria murmured. Jenna had also had a special contact lens fabricated for her right eye, which she'd use to gain entrance. "You must have people in high places."

The clan-lady looked her way before arching an eyebrow. "I have them in *strategic* places." She paused then. "The pass we've given you should get you into the lab without difficulty … the rest will be up to you."

Aria nodded. They'd done their research: Platinum 5's Delta deck housed the Mir-Ferrin military and research facilities. Her pass would get her into the virology lab, but she still hadn't come up with how to escape the space station. Scheduled flights would likely be canceled for a few days after she destroyed the bacteria, while they hunted down the culprit. So, if she couldn't depart immediately, she might have to lie low for a while and then board a passenger liner when the dust had settled.

*If* it settled.

"Your disguise should fool the immigration officials at least," Jenna said. She huffed a wry laugh. "Ardex is certainly better than the face paint and clay Malik and I used to get off Aura Terminal."

Aria inclined her head. She knew that Lady Jenna and her bodyguard had narrowly escaped assassins a year earlier and managed to flee the border station—but she hadn't heard how they'd done it. "What did you disguise yourselves as?"

"Daksari … the face paint and clay were crude but effective."

Aria pulled a face. She was relieved her disguise was more substantial. She'd be wearing a mask made of Ardex, and traveling as a female Nandoon. She had the height to carry it off and had been shocked at how realistic her disguise was when she'd tried it on that morning.

Lady Jenna had also provided Aria with a PCSD loaded with enough credits to buy her way off Platinum 5. The funds would certainly come in useful.

The two women lapsed into silence then, turning the corner and heading down the northern walkway.

Glancing over the railing, and through the clear walls of the walkway, Aria viewed the open-air courtyard five levels below. Her gaze alighted on a figure wielding a laser-blade. Her pace slowed when she recognized the slender woman with black hair.

Dressed in close-fitting black body armor, her hair pulled back into a braid, Isla feinted and parried as the exercise-drone—a blue-grey metallic globe with two antennae protruding like ears—darted around. Intermittently, it sent out slender darts of blue laser, which Isla had to defend herself against.

Aria drew to a halt, watching Isla practice. "She's good," she murmured.

"She is," Jenna agreed. However, the edge to the clan-lady's voice made Aria tear her gaze from the woman below and focus on her instead. The clan-lady was frowning, her jaw tense. "Ever since Cathal's death, Isla has retreated into her own world … one none of us, even her daughter, can reach."

Aria glanced down at the courtyard once more, to see Isla catch a blue arrow on her arm. The exercise-droid was set for 'sparring', which meant it delivered a shock—nothing too strong, but discomforting, nonetheless. Isla's face twisted. "She does seem … detached," she admitted.

It was true: during mealtimes, Isla had little to say. Her blue eyes were often unfocused, as if she was lost in her thoughts.

Jenna nodded, her mouth compressing. "I worry about her sometimes. We all miss Cathal … but Isla won't let him go."

Aria watched Isla drop and roll to avoid another attack. "Where did she learn to fight like that?"

"She's a Mir-Galbreth … there isn't one among them who doesn't learn physical combat from a young age."

Aria nodded. The Mir-Galbreths were warriors—over the centuries, the clan had produced some of the sector's, and indeed the galaxy's, best fighters.

"After she married my brother, Isla stopped her training," Jenna continued. "But soon after we arrived on Staturine II, she picked it up again … she works out twice a day now." The clan-lady turned to Aria then, her mahogany gaze settling upon her. "Enough about my sister-in-law," she said with a rueful smile. "Let's focus on you, Aria. Do you have everything you need for your mission?"

Aria nodded, even as her stomach fluttered nervously. "I believe so … thanks to you."

Lady Jenna huffed a laugh. However, Aria caught the edge to it. "As Vic so eloquently put it … I've got the easy part, 'master-minding' everything from afar."

Aria tensed at the mention of Vic. Since their argument that fateful evening, they hadn't seen each other. Things had gone into a downward spiral when he confronted her, and they'd both said things that couldn't be taken back. Aria didn't even know if he was still on Staturine II. "He was only looking out for me."

"I know … that's why I didn't take offense." Digging into a pocket inside the long gold and black cloak she wore, the clan-lady produced a wrist-comm. "I have something else for you … hold out your arm."

Aria did as bid, watching as Jenna strapped the device around her wrist. "It looks like a standard-issue comm," she went on. "But it also gives you direct access to me." She glanced up then, her gaze spearing Aria's. "I can have a shuttle fetch you from any corner of this sector … all you have to do is ask."

Aria swallowed to ease the sudden tightness in her throat. "You can't send a Mir-Brennan shuttle to Platinum 5 … they'll shoot it down."

Jenna's mouth kicked up into a smile, although her gaze remained sharp. "No … but when you make it off the station, you're going to be hunted. I want to make sure you never get caught." The clan-lady paused there, both her hands closing over Aria's outstretched one. "There will always be a place among my people for you, Aria. When you return from Platinum 5, I'd welcome you as part of my household. There's a research institute here in Briscay … you can have any position you want."

Warmth spread across Aria's chest. Clearing her throat, she managed a weak smile. "You talk as if I'm coming back," she murmured.

Jenna's expression tightened. "I know Vic thinks this is a suicide run … but I don't. You're well prepared, Aria. All you need to do is keep your nerve."

Aria nodded. She felt brave now—but she hoped she would when the heat was on too. "Don't worry … I know what's at stake," she murmured.

Silence fell then, while Jenna studied her face, her expression altering.

"You and Vic," she murmured. "Is there something between you?"

Aria's spine snapped straight, and she stepped back, gently extricating her hand from Jenna's.

The conversation kept coming back to him—and she wished it wouldn't.

She didn't want to think about Vic Mir-Riorde right now. Every time she did, it felt as if a stone had taken up residence in her stomach.

The clan-lady's question was gently spoken, yet it stung like a slap across the face.

Aria shook her head. "Not anymore," she replied softly.

The shunt slid through the wide streets of Briscay, wending its way to the spaceport. Seated near the front of the surface transporter, Aria took in the lofty dove-grey buildings rising toward the sky, towering above the streets and the crowds of warmly dressed citizens who went about their daily life.

The city was much busier than her home one. Many of the buildings housed big galactic corporations and banks. However, as they traveled farther from the business district, Aria caught sight of a huge, gleaming edifice with the words: The Briscay Virology, Immunology, and Pathology Research Institute.

Her pulse quickened.

Jenna had offered her a job here, a future.

Ever since she'd fled Haliaen, she'd been an outcast. And if she managed to destroy the Starellusbacter, she'd be a fugitive.

But the Mir-Brennan clan-lady had offered her sanctuary, freedom.

She had something waiting for her on the other side, something to grasp onto.

*I'll come back*, she promised herself, resolve galvanizing within her. Aria's fingers clenched around the small purse she carried. She'd cast aside her backpack, as it belonged to Aria Mir-Straken, not Varussa Mir-Barus—a Nandoon biologist. Dressed in the flowing purple robes favored by Nandoon females, her mask in place, she had assumed her new identity.

The shunt drew to a smooth halt then, pulling up before a huge, low-slung grey and black building: Briscay's spaceport.

Rising to her feet and retrieving her small trolley suitcase, Aria disembarked with the other passengers and entered the terminal. The departure board hovered above a milling sea of travelers, and she halted, craning her neck to scan it.

The noon flight to Cadex 12 was due to leave in half an hour. She'd already purchased a ticket and checked in. Her case was small enough to carry on, so she only had to go through security.

Lowering her gaze from the holo-screen, Aria scanned the surrounding crowd. Anxiety fluttered up under her ribcage, for she almost expected to see towering bronze battle-droids striding through the terminal, knocking travelers out of the way as they clove a path toward her.

But Vic had removed the tracking device from her back—Elijah had no idea where she was—and she was in disguise. Even if one of her fiancé's battle-droids was to march up to her right now, it would never recognize her.

Recalling the bug that had been implanted in her back was a mistake, for it reminded her of her father … and Vic.

Where was he right now?

Aria's pulse quickened then. She hadn't gone looking for him before her departure, hadn't said goodbye. There was no point.

But he hadn't sought her out either.

Enough. She had to stop thinking about Vic. It was pointless. She had a job to do.

Jaw clenched, Aria strode toward the security gates.

"Where is Aria?"

Obsidian's raspy greeting made Vic tense. "What do you mean?" he asked tersely.

"I understood the female was traveling with us."

Vic slid into the pilot's chair and started doing preflight cheeks, even as irritation bubbled up. "I don't know why you came to that conclusion," he muttered. "She was only catching a lift with us … until we got her to safety."

"So, she will be residing on Staturine II now?"

"Yes." Vic cut the battle-droid a look. Instead, of concentrating on its preflight checks, Obsidian's blood-red gaze was focused on him. He didn't understand why the droid was suddenly so interested in Aria. Nevertheless, over the years they'd worked together, there had been times when he'd wondered if Obsidian's reprogramming hadn't gone deeper than he realized.

Occasionally, the battle-droid came out with statements that surprised him.

Frowning, Vic tried to concentrate on checking the cockpit switches and valves were all in their correct positions and settings. Satisfied, he glanced up to find his first mate still watching him.

Obsidian wasn't content with that answer.

Vic heaved a sigh. "Aria will be going to Platinum 5 to destroy the Starellusbacter."

"Are we assisting her?"

Vic shook his head. He didn't want to talk about Aria. Every time he thought about the final, harsh words that had passed between them, his chest hurt. He'd been attempting to help her, to look out for her, but she'd turned on him.

Sure, he'd been a little heavy-handed—maybe a bit too aggressive. However, he'd been frustrated that he was the only one who seemed to think Jenna's idea was crazy. The clan-lady was sending Aria to her death, yet no one seemed to care.

His gut clenched then. *Hypocrite.* As Aria had so succinctly pointed out, he too had put her life at risk for his own personal benefit. Was he in a position to point the finger at anyone else?

"Has Lady Jenna provided her with a team?"

"No … she's going in alone."

The droid's gaze never wavered. "Will she not be in danger?"

"Most likely." A sickly sensation swept over Vic then. "But it was her choice."

"Did you not offer her—?"

"For fuck's sake," he muttered, his temper fraying. What was wrong with his copilot this morning? Obsidian was never this chatty or annoying. The battle-droid had remained onboard *The Wayfarer* while he'd been visiting the clan-lady; it clearly had missed human company. "Aria doesn't need our help." Reaching forward, Vic punched a series of buttons. The freighter's engines rumbled to life. "Now, let's change the subject."

# 18. RIGHTEOUS AND DEVOTED

ARIA HAD A window seat. Gazing through the layers of tempered glass at Staturine II, she caught her reflection in the window and jolted. She wasn't yet used to her disguise. A stranger stared back at her: a Nandoon with leathery grey-blue skin; a large proboscis; small, deep-set eyes; and a thick neck covered in fleshy wattles. Over the Ardex mask, she wore a curly black wig. She also wore Ardex gloves, to disguise her human hands.

"All passengers, please check your harness is securely fastened." A dispassionate voice vibrated through the large cabin filled with rows of seats, intruding on her inspection of her reflection. "We are about to make the jump into hyperspace."

Aria exhaled sharply and closed her eyes.

Moments later, the engines changed note, the hum and throb beneath her feet altering, and then she was thrown back in her seat.

When she opened her eyes, the stars outside the windows were steaking past.

"This is your captain speaking." Another voice, this one warmer, filled the cabin. "Welcome onboard this flight to Cadex 12. Your flight today will be twelve hours and fifteen minutes. Please sit back and enjoy our selection of in-flight entertainment. The first meal of the journey will be served shortly."

Aria swallowed hard, willing her sudden queasiness to subside. It wasn't space sickness, but nerves.

And a heavy sense of finality.

*I'll never see Vic again.*

She sucked in a deep breath, fighting the sudden tightness in her throat. Initially, after their argument, she'd been furious with him. Their war of words had ended with her storming off to her bedchamber. He hadn't come after her—not that she'd expected him to, especially after the parting insult she'd hurled at him as she went—and the next morning, he'd vacated his bedchamber early.

At the time, she'd felt vindicated, but now regret crushed her chest.

She wished she'd seen him one last time, that she'd swallowed her pride and sought him out so they could have parted on good terms, at least.

She should have made things right. But it was too late now.

"This is an honor, indeed, My Lord." The white-coated man dipped his head, closing the freezer. "Although, if I'd have known you were paying us a visit, I'd have called the whole virology team in so they could meet you."

"No need for that, Doctor," Elijah replied, ignoring the note of censure in the older man's voice. He'd deliberately come to Platinum 5's virology laboratory without telling anyone first.

Not even his younger brother.

Lucas had recently hired Varis Mir-Ferrin to lead the team of scientists, and although his brother provided him with weekly reports, Elijah wanted to see his research for himself.

Varis raised his head, pale grey eyes glinting. "Would you like a tour, My Lord?"

"Yes, thank you."

The lead scientist drew himself up. "I'd be delighted." He made an expansive gesture with his hand. "As you can see, we're currently standing in the general laboratory area."

Elijah nodded, his gaze traveling over the functional space lined with safety hoods, pipettes, centrifuges, fridges, and freezers. It wasn't a pleasant working environment but soulless and sterile. The air was sharp with the odor of disinfectant, the hum of the life-support surrounding them.

The harsh overhead lights gleamed off Varis's shiny forehead as he moved through the laboratory, pointing out items of interest.

"Of course, our laboratory is organized into functional areas," the scientist went on. "To provide a safe and effective environment that ensures our testing is as accurate as possible."

The man sounded as if he was reciting from a manual, and Elijah gave a thin smile. If he hadn't met Aria, he'd have thought all scientists were as dry as this one.

He tensed then, his brow furrowing.

His fiancée had truly vanished. The team he'd sent to retrieve her hadn't turned up any leads in days now.

Maybe it was time for him to accept the truth.

Aria had fled rather than marry him. He thought they'd been friends, that their relationship was one based on mutual respect. But her apparent willingness to unite their clans had been a ruse. She'd waited until their wedding day but hadn't been able to go through with it.

Elijah's jaw tightened, his mood souring. He couldn't continue hunting Aria forever. What would he do if he found her—drag her back to Platinum 5 in chains?

"This is our specimen collection and preparation area," Varis went on, gesturing to a narrow corridor that led off the main laboratory. "And we conduct our molecular virology and serology experiments in those two labs down there." He pointed to the twin doors at the far end of the lab before turning to Elijah, a proud smile on his face. He gestured behind the clan-lord. "We also have a virus and bacteria culture isolation unit."

Elijah turned to see a set of heavy windowed doors. Through the glass, he spied a pair of lab techs—masks, goggles, and suits in place—working with microscopes.

"Is that where you're conducting our 'special' project?"

Tension rippled across Varis's face, and he glanced around nervously. There weren't many technicians in the lab this morning, although the lead scientist's reaction revealed that Lucas's research wasn't common knowledge here.

"Yes, My Lord," he murmured. "We keep the Starellusbacter in there."

"Who knows about the project?" Elijah asked, his tone casual.

"Just me and two technicians." Varis nodded to the two figures inside the lab. "Enis Mir-Ferrin and Tyrell Mir-Hydra."

Elijah took a mental note of the names; Lucas had been vague about such details, but if Elijah was sanctioning this research, he wished to know everything about it, including whom they'd hired to work on the bacteria.

"Can we go inside the isolation unit?" Elijah asked.

Varis's shoulders tensed, although, after a moment, he nodded. "Yes, My Lord … but we'll have to suit up."

Elijah's mouth quirked. "So be it."

"There it is."

The pride in Varis Mir-Ferrin's voice was impossible to miss. However, Elijah wasn't focused on him, but on the drawer of covered agar media plates that one of the lab techs had just opened for him. Neat rows of samples—mottled brown markings against a red culture—lay before him.

A shiver rippled down Elijah's spine.

It was hard to imagine how something so small could be so deadly. Nonetheless, Lucas had described to him, with great zeal too, just how the Starellusbacter worked. It attacked the lungs first, causing severe breathing difficulties within just a few hours of being infected. It then moved on to the central nervous system, and seizures and death followed.

"How is work proceeding on a cure for it?" he asked after a pause.

"Has your brother not been keeping you informed?"

Elijah glanced at Varis then. He couldn't see his expression under the mask he wore, yet he marked how the man's pale eyes narrowed behind his safety glasses.

"Naturally," Elijah drawled, holding the man's gaze, "but I wish to have an update, directly from you, Doctor."

Varis glanced at one of his assistants before his attention shifted back to the clan-lord. "It still resists all known antibiotics," he admitted, his tone sullen, "but we're making progress."

"We're likely to find a cure within the next month, My Lord," one of the techs said eagerly. Elijah took note of the badge on the young man's chest: Tyrell Mir-Hydra. Next to him, his female companion remained silent, while Varis shot him a warning look.

"That's promising," Elijah replied, keeping his voice carefully neutral.

In truth, this whole enterprise gave him cold sweats.

He'd initially agreed to Lucas proceeding with his research project, one that had already been sanctioned by their father, but with the passing of the days, and weeks, since, thoughts about this super-bacterium, and the damage it could wreak, preyed on his mind and made his sleep fitful.

He was allowing the project to continue, yet he wished to know more about the monster they'd created.

"Are these all the samples?" he asked, gesturing to the drawer of Petri dishes.

"These are our newest ones," Tyrell answered before Varis had a chance. The young technician was eager to impress his clan-lord it seemed. "All the others are stored in there." He pointed to a freezer against the wall.

Elijah nodded, glancing back at Varis.

The lead scientist had gone still, and the glint in his eyes warned that the man didn't welcome his questions or Tyrell's eager responses.

"I'm paying for this research, Doctor," Elijah said, his tone hardening. "And if these bacteria are as deadly as you claim, I'd feel better knowing exactly where you're keeping every last sample."

A hollow silence followed before Varis eventually cleared his throat. "Of course, My Lord." His tone was obsequious, yet brittle. "Rest assured that every sample we have of Starellusbacter … fresh and frozen … is in here."

# 19. ONE STEP AT A TIME

THERE WASN'T MUCH to see on Cadex 12. The space station was a sector hub, positioned at the intersection between Mir-Brennan, Mir-Lelith, and Mir-Ferrin territories. It was an interchange, a hulking grey-blue hive orbiting a tawny gas giant.

Few people visited Cadex 12 for pleasure, and neither was Aria. Like most, she was just passing through.

Disembarking from the passenger liner that had brought her from Staturine II, she walked through the vast terminal, toward the gate where her connecting flight to Platinum 5 was due to leave shortly.

A crowd of passengers had already gathered before the gate, while two utility-droids prepared to open up boarding for the flight. Joining the throng, Aria glanced around her. Now that she was halfway through her journey, the nerves had really set in.

She'd barely been able to eat during the previous flight. Her stomach cramped every time she thought about what lay ahead, and she'd made far too many visits to the bathroom.

Sweat beaded on her forehead now when she caught sight of the Mir-Ferrin clan insignia—a crescent moon and twin crossed blades, with the motto 'Righteous and devoted' beneath it—on the sleek arrowhead-shaped liner parked beyond the windows.

*Righteous and devoted*—it summed up the Mir-Ferrins. They were fierce and loyal, qualities she'd admired until recently. But engineering a bacterium that could wipe out whole planets had destroyed the respect she'd once had for Elijah and his family.

She'd known Mican Mir-Ferrin and his sons were ruthless, yet this was next level.

Lady Jenna was right—they had to be stopped.

Aria's pulse accelerated, and she drew in a deep, steadying breath.

*Keep calm*, she counseled herself. At this rate, she'd be a sweaty, palpitating wreck by the time they docked at Platinum 5. *Take this one step at a time.*

Settling down into her seat and clipping on her harness, Aria silently repeated the mantra. *One step at a time.*

It was best she didn't look too far ahead, that she focused only on what had to be achieved in each stage of her plan. Even so, she was shaky and on edge. It didn't help that she was exhausted. She hadn't slept at all during the first leg of the trip. However, once they'd taken off and made the jump into hyperspace, she'd retire to the berth she'd reserved, where she'd be able to shower and stretch out for a few hours.

The journey to Platinum 5 was a long one, nearly twenty hours.

The engines rumbled to life, and Aria sucked in another deep breath, her gaze dropping to where her hands sat clenched upon her lap. The gleaming surface of her wrist-comm winked up at her then, a reminder that Lady Jenna was providing her with a means of disappearing once she got off Platinum 5.

Unfortunately, she'd started to worry about how she was going to achieve that.

Vic wasn't wrong about the level of risk she was taking on—even if she managed to destroy the Starellusbacter, escaping the station could be difficult.

Heat ignited in her belly then, stubbornness steadying her jittery nerves.

It was just as well that she was resourceful.

She had a plan of Platinum 5 and a detailed one of the virology lab on her tablet—an encrypted, password-protected file, just in case anyone scanned her device. The pass and special contact lens she carried were tucked away in her bag.

Aria had already studied both plans carefully. The Mir-Ferrin biological research institute sat in the midst of the station's Delta deck, but the virology laboratory sat apart from it. Once she entered the lab, she'd have to work fast. The bacteria would be housed in the isolation unit, which was also fitted with autoclaves and a vaporizer.

Aria inhaled slowly then. *One step at a time*, she reminded herself once more.

It was an irony that she was heading to Platinum 5, while her fiancé was still hunting her. Elijah had no idea she'd soon be right under his nose.

*Elijah.*

She'd deliberately avoided thinking about him on this trip so far. Tension rippled through her then as she recalled the terrifying battle-droids he'd sent after her.

Whatever the reason for her jilting him, he hadn't needed to pursue her like that.

She'd thought Elijah was her friend, yet in the end, he wasn't that different to her father. To him, she was nothing more than a possession.

She was his bride-to-be, and he wanted her back.

Aria's jaw firmed, her gaze going to the window as the passenger liner slid out of the landing bay.

*Over my dead body.*

Aria stirred awake, lying there for a few moments in blissful oblivion.

For an instant or two, she forgot where she was or what had brought her here—and then the memories returned, crashing over her like rough waves, throwing her back onto the shore.

Groaning, she rolled over onto her back and opened her eyes, staring up at the silver-blue panels of the low ceiling. Her berth was cramped, with plain metal walls and floor, and furnished with little more than a single bed and a nightstand. The room had an ensuite bathroom that was so tiny it felt as if it had been made for Gibbits rather than humans.

Even so, Aria had been relieved to be able to retreat to her own private space for a few hours—to stand under stinging needles of hot water for a few minutes before crawling onto her bed. She'd fallen asleep within minutes of lying down.

Rubbing her gritty eyes, she peered at her wrist-comm. She'd been asleep ten hours.

With a sigh, Aria pushed herself up, swinging her legs over the side of her bed, and wincing as her bare feet hit the cold metal floor.

*Back to reality.*

Thoughts of Vic crept in then, unbidden. She'd done her best to distract herself, to focus on other things during this journey, yet worries crowded in now that her defenses were lowered briefly.

Where had he gone after leaving Staturine II? Presumably, he was keen to offload those hyperdrives and find his next job.

A familiar ache rose under her breastbone as she imagined him and Obsidian sitting side by side in the cockpit of *The Wayfarer*. Hopefully, he'd give Calberic a wide berth in future. He'd never be welcome in Fort Elisik again.

Aria muttered a curse then. Why was she concerned about him?

Her own fate was far more precarious.

Her belly rumbled then, reminding her that it had been hours since she'd eaten anything. Finally, she had her appetite back, and should eat before nerves twisted her gut in knots again.

Going to the bathroom, she pulled on her Ardex mask and wig. The thick rubbery material was hot and itchy on her face, but she was going to have to get used to it. Satisfied her mask was in place, she dressed, donning her flowing purple robes once more, and her Ardex gloves.

Leaving her berth, Aria made her way back to the large cabin.

The aroma of roast meat, gravy, and spices drifted her way then, and Aria's mouth filled with saliva.

Returning to her seat, Aria called a droid and ordered a large meal. While she waited for it to arrive, she surveyed the cabin. They'd dimmed the lights. Some travelers, who couldn't afford a berth, slumped in their seats, although many places, including the row Aria sat in, were empty.

Aria was tempted to dig into her bag, retrieve her tablet, and resume her study of the plan of the virology lab.

However, if she focused on that right now, she'd likely lose her appetite again.

Instead, Aria settled for staring out the window at the streaming river of stars until the droid brought her a tray.

She ate slowly, which was a necessity anyway with her mask on. As flexible as the Ardex was, it hampered the movements of her jaw a little. She savored the braised Fer-beast steak—accompanied by pureed root vegetables and a delicious bread studded with nuts— and sipped a glass of red wine. Dessert was a light mousse flavored with Mandoli, a spice from her world, Haliaen.

The flavor transported her back to her childhood, to dinners with her parents before her mother had sickened and died. Before her already distant father withdrew to a place she couldn't reach him. To happier times than these.

Eyes stinging, Aria put down her spoon, leaving the dessert unfinished. Damn it, couldn't she even enjoy her last meal before Platinum 5? Why couldn't the past stay buried?

A utility-droid wheeled past, collecting her tray. However, Aria kept her glass of wine, sipping it slowly while she switched on the vid-screen on the seat in front of her. They couldn't access any live newsfeeds while a craft was in hyperspace, but she'd been out of things of late.

It was time she caught up on the news.

After five minutes of watching the lead stories, she wished she hadn't.

The Mir-Leliths had just rejected a new proposal by the Mir-Brennans to share mining rights for Staturine II. Their representative announced that the revised trade agreement was still 'an insult' to their clan.

Aria pulled a face at this news. She then continued to scan the feed.

Pirate raids had increased on the fringes of the sector, with two Mir-Ferrin border-patrol ships attacked.

To top it off, there had been a local uprising on Idral—one that had been violently quelled by the new Mir-Ferrin governor.

Aria switched off the vid-screen. It was a litany of depressing and worrying news. The Rith Sector was weathering unstable times. That was why pirates grew increasingly bold. Chaos thrived when the clans went to war.

Raising her glass to her lips, Aria drained the last of her wine. She considered ordering another. She wasn't usually much of a drinker, but she needed something to settle her nerves. If she were onboard *The Wayfarer*, Vic would have offered her a tumbler of Morith whisky right now.

She tensed.

Thinking about *The Wayfarer* was a mistake, for it just brought her thoughts back to Vic. An image of them seated opposite each other sharing a drink together after they'd fled Lanthor returned. She hadn't been sure about the whisky, but she'd enjoyed their conversation.

Even then, she'd been fascinated by him.

Aria's fingers tightened around the stem of her empty glass. *For the love of the Gods, stop it*. Maybe she would order something stronger than wine, just not a shot of Morith whisky. Anything but that. They still had a few hours until Platinum 5—she'd arrive sober.

Aria was just about to reach up and press the button above her head to call a droid when a familiar voice made her freeze.

"Want some company?"

# 20. THE MACHINE INSIDE ME

ARIA TWISTED LEFT, her gaze alighting on a tall, well-built male figure. The black and silver plate over his right eye socket glinted in the dim cabin lights. Dressed in charcoal pants, shirt, and cloak, he carried a small duffel bag slung over one shoulder.

Aria gasped, her heart kicking hard against her ribs. "What are you doing here?"

Vic stared down at her, his mouth twitching. "Keeping you out of trouble."

"But how—" she motioned to her disguised face "—did you know—"

"I made a call to Lady Jenna," he murmured.

"You've forgiven her then?"

A nerve flickered in his cheek. "Not exactly," he admitted, his voice roughening. "But I realize she's acting in the best interests of her clan. It just came as a shock … that's all."

Aria held his gaze, her pulse still hammering. An odd sense of disconnection flooded over her and made her feel light-headed. She'd spent the better part of this trip telling herself she'd never see this man ever again—but here he was.

"You'd better sit down," she said finally. Her voice came out strangled, but she couldn't help it. She was still reeling.

He nodded, dropping into the seat at the end of the row and placing his duffel bag next to him. There were two spaces between them, which was just as well because Aria was still coming to terms with the fact that he was here. She didn't want him too close.

A droid appeared next to Vic then, lights blinking. "Can I take your glass?" it chirped.

"Yes, thank you." Aria passed Vic her glass so the droid could take it.

"Would you like anything else?"

"No thanks," Vic replied.

The utility-droid moved off, leaving the pair of them alone once again.

Swallowing hard, to ease the sudden tightness in her throat, Aria studied Vic's face, wishing he could give her some clue to his thoughts.

"I don't understand," she whispered finally. "Why would you follow me?"

Vic leaned back in his seat before glancing her way. "I can't let you do this on your own, Aria," he said softly. This corner of the cabin was largely deserted as most of the passengers had retired to their berths for the moment. Nevertheless, she was grateful he kept his voice down.

She frowned, even as her chest constricted. "You don't think me capable?"

"I know you are up to it," he replied without hesitation. "And I know you're prepared ... but you need someone watching your back. And you need a solid escape plan."

Aria stared back at him for a moment before she cleared her throat. "We shouldn't be discussing this here," she murmured. "I've booked a berth ... let's take this conversation there."

Vic leaned up against the cool metal wall inside the cramped berth, his gaze settling upon the woman perched on the edge of the bed.

Aria had removed her mask and gloves. Just as well, for it was disconcerting looking at her twitching proboscis and quivering wattles; the disguise was convincing, indeed.

However, now he could see her face, Vic tensed. Aria's jaw was set, her fingers clenched together upon her lap.

Vic sucked in a deep breath and shifted his attention to the silver-blue paneled wall behind her. He wasn't doing a great job of explaining himself.

There was a volcano simmering away inside him, yet whenever he opened his mouth, his words sounded cold and flat.

He refocused on Aria then, to find her watching him, her emerald gaze veiled. She looked unhappy. He didn't like seeing her like this.

"You don't always need to come to my rescue, Vic," she said then, her voice brittle. "I'm not your responsibility."

He let out a sharp exhale before raking a hand through his hair. He then breathed a curse.

Aria's gaze snapped wide. "Excuse me?"

"I'm useless at this," he muttered. "I know you don't need a hero, Aria … but I'm sorry for the way things ended between us on Staturine II. I was too aggressive."

She sighed, her shoulders slumping. "You were … but I also let my temper get the best of me. I apologize for the things I said … I didn't mean any of them."

Something deep inside his chest unknotted at this admission.

"I've regretted our fight ever since," she added.

"So have I," he murmured. It was all Vic had thought about over the past days. "I don't know how to be close to anyone, Aria. I could blame the transitioning, but I know better. Even before that pirate shot me in the chest, I had trouble expressing myself. Emotions aren't my strong suit … they never have been."

She stared back at him, her gaze widening.

"I tried to walk away, you know?" he admitted hoarsely. "I tried to leave you behind me."

She swallowed. "What stopped you?"

"Obsidian. He made a fuss about letting you go off alone … he just wouldn't shut up. My first mate seems to think we three are a team now … he kept asking why I'd abandoned you."

Aria's mouth quirked at this admission. "Where are Obsidian and *The Wayfarer* now?"

"I left them both on Cadex 12." Vic sucked in a deep breath then. He had to get these words out. "It's a shock to discover a droid has more humanity than you do." His throat constricted, goosebumps rising on his skin. "I can't let the machine inside me take over, Aria. I have nanobots keeping my immune system working, wires coiled through my brain, synth blood running through my veins … and a regulator that keeps my heart pumping." He paused then, a sickly sensation flooding over him. He didn't like to dwell on what he was, on what they'd done to him. "I don't want to spend the rest of my life alone, unable to forge relationships … running whenever things get tough."

Silence settled then.

Wordlessly, Aria rose to her feet and stepped forward, closing in on him. However, she halted when they were a couple of feet apart. She held his gaze, her full lips parting. "You're not running now," she whispered. "And for the record, Vic, there's more humanity in you than in anyone I've ever met."

Vic inhaled deeply, breathing in the sweet scent of her skin and the floral notes of the shampoo or bodywash she'd recently used. His stomach dropped, need clenching hard inside him.

He reached out and took her hand, cradling it in his own. Her pulse hammered against his fingertips. Aria wasn't any calmer than he was right now, and the realization eased his nerves.

"I've always found actions easier than words," he admitted. "And I'm still not expressing myself properly. We haven't known each other long, but you matter to me, Aria … and that's why I'm here."

He drew her hand up, his lips brushing the fluttering pulse on her inner wrist.

She gave a soft gasp, and when he met her gaze once more, Aria's pupils had dilated. Her chest rose and fell sharply. "I don't want to put you in danger," she said, her voice catching. "I'm risking my own neck, but I don't want to risk yours."

"Let me worry about my neck," he murmured back, brushing his lips over her pulse once more.

He drew her toward him then, closing the remaining gap between them.

Aria came willingly, and when his arms closed around her, when his mouth came down on hers, a sigh of surrender gusted from her.

Vic swallowed it.

He kissed her slowly, deeply, emotion wrenching in his chest.

Aria melted against him, and he ran his hands down her back, tracing the long arch of her spine before he cupped her lush backside, pulling her against him. Aria moaned low in her throat, raising her arms to link them around his neck. She pushed her breasts against his chest, undulating her hips against him.

Vic deepened the kiss, his tongue stroking hers.

When he eventually drew back, they were both panting.

"I'd better stop," he ground out, even as his groin throbbed in protest. "Or I'll lose it."

Aria's mouth curved, her gaze glinting. "Go on," she whispered. "Lose it."

She stepped back from him then and removed the purple cloak from about her shoulders, tossing it carelessly onto the floor. After that, she kicked off her shoes and began to wriggle out of her robes.

Vic's heart started pounding. His self-control unraveled, lust spiking through his gut, his cock jerking against his pants. He shrugged off his cloak and heeled off his boots.

Moments later, they were both naked.

Vic pushed Aria back on the narrow bed, climbing over her. He grabbed her wrists then, pinning them above her head, while his mouth claimed hers once more. Their kisses turned wild, their teeth clashing, tongues dueling—and then Vic grazed his lips down her jaw and throat, nipping, licking, and kissing as he went.

Her magnificent, dusky-tipped breasts thrust up to meet his hungry mouth.

He suckled her, gently at first, before he let himself go, drawing each hard tip deep into his mouth.

Aria gasped and groaned under him.

Her reaction made him hungry for more. She had a luscious body, one to rival Miradia, the Goddess of Fertility. He wanted to devour her.

Releasing her wrists, Vic shifted down, his mouth exploring the curve of her belly, his tongue tracing the indentation of her navel before he spread her trembling thighs wide and gazed down at her.

Aria breathed his name, and he glanced up at her face. Her eyes were hooded, her lips parted.

"Gods, I want you so much," he croaked.

"Take me … I'm yours," she whispered.

Vic shifted back, parting her wider still and lowering himself between her thighs. "You are," he replied, letting his breath feather her skin. He tasted her then, his hands sliding under her backside, gripping her tightly as he lifted her up to meet his hungry mouth.

Aria's whimper filled the small room, and she bucked against him, caught by surprise as his tongue flicked and delved. But he held her fast. He started suckling her as he had her breasts, and Aria cried out, writhing on the bed, and clutching at him.

He kept going, insistent, relentless, until she eventually shattered against his tongue.

Vic gently lowered her onto the bed and sat back on his heels, his gaze roaming the glistening curves of her sweat-slicked body.

He'd thought her beautiful before, but he wanted this vision of her imprinted on his mind to his dying day: Aria spread out before him, undone.

Yet he wasn't finished with her.

Taking hold of her left leg, and hooking his arm under the knee, he positioned the swollen head of his cock at her entrance.

A heartbeat later, he drove into her, sheathing himself to the hilt.

Aria gasped and lifted her pelvis off the bed once more, angling herself up to bring him deeper still.

Heat pulsed at the base of Vic's spine, tension gathering, yet he gritted his teeth, holding himself in check. Being inside this woman was like nothing else he'd ever experienced, but he wanted to make it last, for them both.

He held himself over her, and slowly withdrew, savoring the slick slide. The musky scent of her arousal made him light-headed with lust. He felt as if he'd just downed half a bottle of Morith whisky. He felt powerful too, as if nothing could ever touch him while he was buried deep inside her.

He took her in slow, deep thrusts, watching pleasure ripple over Aria's face every time he slid home.

Sweat slicked both their bodies now, and Vic's arms started to shake as tension gathered within him like a storm.

Jaw clenched, he continued to ride her, rotating his hips now to change the angle.

Aria's choked cry greeted him, and a wet rush of heat enveloped his shaft. She trembled under him, her head falling back against the pillow—and Vic let himself go, thrusting into her savagely until his spine snapped back, and his own, feral, cry echoed against the metal walls of the berth.

# 21. MAKING PLANS

"SYR, HAVE MERCY," Aria sighed, trailing her fingertips down Vic's damp chest. "I don't think I'm going to be able to walk after this."

He looked down at her, his hazel eye shadowing. "I got carried away," he murmured. "Did I hurt you?"

Aria stared up at him, her throat tightening at the concern in his gaze. Of course, she often forgot his bionic strength. He worried that he might accidentally harm her. "No," she whispered, her hand rising to his face and cupping his cheek. "Not in the slightest. It was …" Her voice trailed off, as she struggled to find the words to express herself.

In truth, she was still reeling after what they'd done, after the way he'd kissed, touched, and taken her. Her climax had been so powerful, she'd felt as if she'd been flung halfway across the galaxy and was now slowly orbiting a distant sun. Her body was molten, her limbs loose. She wanted to hold onto the intensity, but already she could feel reality pressing in, reminding her that these moments couldn't last.

In just a handful of hours, they'd be docking upon Platinum 5.

But right now, they were here, in each other's arms. She didn't want to let go of this moment.

"Life changing," Vic said then, finishing her sentence, his mouth twitching. Whenever his lips did that, she knew he was trying to smile. The transitioning hadn't erased all trace of facial expression, after all.

"Yes," she breathed. That was the right term for it.

They lay sprawled together on the single bed, the warm air from the life-support feathering over their naked skin. Vic had shifted slightly to one side, so as not to crush her, although their limbs were still entangled.

They lapsed into silence then, each withdrawing into their own thoughts as the moments stretched out. A warm sense of well-being cocooned Aria; she'd never felt as at peace with the universe and her place in it.

She knew what lay ahead, and how dangerous it was going to be, but it couldn't cast a shadow over this.

Over them.

But there was no avoiding the future, and eventually, Vic shattered the moment. "So, you're prepared for your arrival on Platinum 5?"

Aria sucked in a deep breath before nodding. "I've been studying the plans Lady Jenna gave me. I've got the clearance I need to get into the virology lab."

Vic propped himself up on an elbow, regarding her. "Do you know exactly where they're keeping the bacteria?"

She nodded. "The lab only has one isolation unit … the Starellusbacter is too dangerous to be stored anywhere else."

"How are you going to get into the unit without arousing suspicion?"

"I won't … the only way is to go in when there's no one else there." She paused then. "Fortunately, Lady Jenna's spy also provided us with the lab shift schedule … there's a window of five hours when the laboratory is empty."

Vic nodded. "Before you go in … we need to have our escape worked out."

She pulled a face. "I still don't have anything sorted for that. However, Lady Jenna has given me a PCSD loaded with credits."

"It's the least she could do," he replied. His gaze then narrowed. "Since this mission was her idea."

Aria didn't reply—there was little point trying to defend the clan-lady's decision—and after a few seconds, his gaze softened. He then brushed the back of his hand over her cheek. "Leave finding our escape route to me."

"You've got some ideas?"

"You forget I grew up on Platinum 5 … it was my home until six years ago." Vic shifted off her and raised his right wrist. "Once we disembark, we'll need to ensure we can keep in contact. We've both got wrist-comms … we just have to sync them and establish a private channel." He paused then. "Switch your screen on."

Aria lifted her wrist, for she hadn't taken off the wrist-comm earlier, and tapped the gleaming surface on the front of her device. An instant later, it lit up, while Vic did the same with his. He then grunted. "It's done … all you have to do is say my full name, and it'll open up a direct, encrypted line to me." His gaze flicked up, seizing hers. "I'm right with you, Aria … every step of the way."

Aria's throat thickened, her vision misting. "I'm glad," she admitted softly. And she was. The idea of having someone on Platinum 5 who was looking out for her, waiting to help her, eased the tangle of nerves in her stomach.

She was going to have to enter the lab alone, but she no longer felt so isolated.

Their gazes held for a moment before Aria swallowed. "We should have a rendezvous point … for afterward."

"We will." His expression shadowed then. "I could lie here with you for a week, Aria … but our time is running out."

She nodded, anxiety clenching its fist in her solar plexus. "Come on then," she murmured. "Let's get dressed, and I'll bring up the plans Lady Jenna gave me."

Peering out of the passenger liner's window, Vic caught sight of Platinum 5 for the first time in over half a decade.

His skin prickled, his breathing quickening.

He'd hoped never to set foot on the station again—in fact, when he'd deserted from Mir-Ferrin space fleet, he'd vowed he wouldn't.

But fate had decided otherwise, and here he was.

All the same, there was no denying Platinum 5 was impressive. A stack of gleaming silver wheels mounted upon a central core, the massive station orbited Formidian, an unhabitable class H planet that was searingly hot, with no surface water.

Platinum 5 sparkled against the void, its bright silver plating reflecting the light of the red dwarf sun Formidian orbited, and as they drew closer, rows of twinkling lights became visible.

Vic's heart started to pound as memories resurfaced. Mostly, they were of people. His parents. His friends. His cohort of marines. Those he'd lost and left behind. Emotions barreled into him too. The despair he'd felt upon waking after surgery, and the panic that had surged when he'd climbed into his pod inside the cyborg hive for the first time. And the desperation that had clawed its way up his throat day after day until he'd deserted.

He'd grown up on this station, had served here—but it no longer represented home.

Dragging in a deep breath, Vic shifted his attention from the window, his gaze traveling four rows forward to where Aria had taken her seat for docking.

They wouldn't risk having any contact with each other from now on. It was safer if they disembarked separately and met up afterward.

Vic exhaled slowly, his mind running through the plans they'd made in the final hours of their journey. Platinum 5 had a great number of landing bays. Once they docked, they'd make their way to the ones where the cargo ships docked and search the private berths for someone willing to get them off the station, no questions asked.

Vic glanced once more out of the window. They were gliding toward the spaceport, located on the lowermost deck of the station. Platinum 5 consisted of five decks—Alpha, Beta, Gamma, Delta, and Omega—rotating slowly upon a central core. Alpha belonged entirely to the clan-lord, his family, and retainers—they'd be avoiding that one. Beta was the administration center and Gamma the business hub, while Delta housed the military barracks and research centers. The bottom level, Omega, was the station's service deck; it was where the spaceport and cargo bays were located.

Being a military brat, Vic had grown up on Delta and then worked there. As a result, he knew exactly where the laboratories were located.

Vic's gaze settled once more on the crown of Aria's head. She was looking out the window at where hangar doors opened to receive the liner.

Suddenly, it felt as if a hand had just reached into his chest and squeezed hard.

Vic struggled against the protective instinct that kicked in whenever Aria was near. If he wasn't careful, it could get them both killed.

He'd made the decision to join Aria, to assist her—but they'd only get off Platinum 5 alive if he didn't let emotion cloud his judgment.

It wasn't easy though. After what they'd recently shared, the things they'd both told each other, he couldn't pretend he didn't care. He didn't want to. The events of the past days had taught him that he wanted Aria Mir-Straken in his life.

Deep in thought, Vic didn't even notice that the liner had smoothly slid into its docking bay. It was only when the captain's cheerful voice blared across the cabin, welcoming everyone to Platinum 5, that he paid attention to his surroundings once more.

Unbuckling his harness, Vic waited while the other passengers in his row vacated their seats and retrieved their hand luggage.

Then he rose from his seat, grabbed his duffel bag from the overhead locker, and followed the crowd off the liner.

Bright lights greeted him, illuminating the white and bronze landing bay in sharp relief, when he stepped out onto the walkway leading into the arrivals terminal. Vic resisted the urge to pull up the hood of his cloak. Mir-Ferrin clan banners were everywhere. Once Vic had proudly donned his bronze uniform, had worn the Mir-Ferrin crescent moon and twin crossed blades on his chest, but these days, the sight of those things seemed to belong to another life. Another man.

At security, the passengers formed orderly lines, splitting into Mir-Ferrin clan members, and everyone else.

Vic joined the latter line, as did Aria. She was a few yards ahead of him, and he watched her halt before the immigration official, flanked by two bronze battle-droids.

Soon it was Aria's turn to step up before them. The female Nandoon halted in front of the security officer, shoulders stooped, her shimmering purple cloak bright against the austere surroundings.

Tense moments passed before the official handed Aria's ID card back to her and waved her on.

Vic's gaze tracked Aria until she disappeared. He was aware then that his heart was racing, sweat beading on his skin.

He sucked in a deep breath, and then another, focusing on lowering his heart rate.

Aria had gotten through. Now it was his turn.

Reaching the head of the line, Vic held out his ID to the official. It was a fake ID, one of a few he'd procured over the years—handy for whenever he ventured into Mir-Ferrin territory, where he was on record as a deserter.

The official, a thin man with a sharp-featured face, compressed his lips as he scrutinized the ID and then held it up to a scanner. Glancing back at Vic, he then studied the ID once more.

"Cad Mir-Drak," he murmured. "It says here you're a tech specialist."

"I am … in bioengineering."

The official's gaze rested upon the metal plate covering Vic's right eye socket. "You've been modified?"

"Yes." Now was one of those times Vic wished he could smile. His blank expression often made officials like this one jumpy. He reached up and tapped his eye plant. "An ultra-fast data processor in the right frontal lobe."

The man's brows drew together. "Why would you pay to make yourself look like a cyborg?"

Vic shrugged, feigning nonchalance, even as his pulse kicked up a notch. The security officer was showing far too much interest in him. "The mod was worth it. My mind has never worked faster ... I recommend it."

The man's mouth compressed, while Vic focused on keeping his breathing slow and even. He was aware of the battle-droids' crimson gazes upon him, pinning him to the ground. One word from the official and they'd haul him away.

Long moments passed before the security officer handed back Vic's ID. "If you say so." He then gave a terse nod. "Move on."

# 22. NO QUESTIONS ASKED

THEY'D AGREED TO meet in the arrivals terminal, under the large holo-screen, where a glowing list of incoming space flights hovered above the crowd. A gleaming bronze floor stretched across the wide terminal, while a vast, clear dome arched overhead, giving incoming travelers a view of the twinkling cosmos.

Standing there, pretending to watch the board, Aria tried not to let nerves get to her. It was hard though.

She'd chanced a look over her shoulder while she'd been in the immigration queue and spied Vic a few yards behind her. However, she had no idea if he'd been held up or not.

Her own fake ID and disguise had gotten her through easily—far easier than she'd expected. The official hadn't even asked her about the nature of her business on Platinum 5. She'd had a story ready, just in case, though.

"Ready to go?"

A familiar voice intruded then, and Aria glanced left to see a cloaked figure standing at her shoulder. Now that he was through immigration and security, Vic had pulled up the hood of his cloak.

Relief weakened Aria's limbs, and she nodded. "Any problems?"

"No more than I expected … come on, let's get out of here."

Side-by-side, they set off toward the exit, weaving their way through the crowd. Aria surveyed her surroundings, her pulse quickening when she spied a glint of bronze armor.

Battle-droids were patrolling the terminal, laser-rifles slung over their shoulders.

She started to sweat then. Of course, they wouldn't recognize her; even so, the sight of them reminded her that this was the heart of Mir-Ferrin territory.

Elijah was likely in residence too.

Lengthening her stride—and careful to keep her shoulders rounded, in the classic Nandoon posture—she loped toward the glass doors leading out of the terminal, stepping onto a wide moving walkway. There were many of these on Platinum 5. Banks of elevators took you up and down the central stem, between levels, while moving walkways constantly circled each deck.

Beyond the terminal, the lighting was so bright it almost hurt her eyes. The interior of Platinum 5 was so starkly white that it was like stepping inside a floodlit ice cave. Splashes of bronze appeared here and there, yet it didn't soften the austerity.

The walkway traveled through a luminous, smooth-sided tunnel. The Mir-Ferrin clan insignia was everywhere, a constant reminder of where they were, and soft, chiming music played in the background.

The walkway moved swiftly, yet Aria and Vic strode along it to speed up their journey. As she walked, Aria spied a number of 'landings' leading off to various residential wards on Omega deck.

The Delta deck, where the virology lab sat, was on the next level up—but Aria wouldn't go up there for a few hours yet.

She and Vic had set their wrist-comms for local time. Although it was a space station, Platinum 5 kept a terrestrial time, in keeping with its thirty-hour orbit around Formidian. The Mir-Ferrins believed doing so kept its citizens' circadian rhythms intact. The last shift at the virology lab ended in six hours when the station went into its artificial night.

In the meantime, Vic had some work to do.

The walkway wasn't crowded; even so, they didn't speak during the journey to the cargo area. Instead, they both scanned their surroundings as they traveled.

They stepped off the walkway in Ward 50 and entered a hub filled with eateries and shops. Like the walkway tunnel, the hub's walls were smooth and gleaming white. On the far side of the space, large bronze doors led through to the private landing and cargo bays.

Aria glanced around her with interest. "I didn't expect to see a space like this down here," she admitted.

"Each ward on Platinum 5 has one of these," Vic murmured, breaking the silence between them as they walked across a paved area. "They service those living on each of the decks."

"It's cheerful," Aria replied, taking in the wide, brightly lit hub. Although they were in an artificial environment, an effort had been made to soften the whiteness and make the recreational and entertainment space a pleasant one. Potted plants with dark, glossy leaves decorated the pristine snow-white floor, and tinkling fountains, dedicated to various galactic Gods, gave an air of calm. Citizens, many of them dressed in white and bronze jumpsuits, moved through the hub.

Vic drew to a halt then before an eatery with a terrace out front. "Can I borrow that PCSD Jenna gave you?"

Aria nodded, unzipping her purse. Of course, if he found a pilot willing to assist him, he'd need to hand over some credits. "Make sure you pay a deposit only," she warned him. "We must—" Aria's voice cut off as she dug around in her purse. "Shit … it's gone!"

"The PCSD?"

Aria nodded. Heart pounding, she opened her purse wide and peered into it. There was no doubt about it, the small, circular device was missing. "Someone must have pickpocketed me."

She glanced up to see Vic's gaze was narrowed. "Where?"

Their gazes met before a sickly sensation washed over her. "The arrivals terminal." She'd stood there for a few minutes, staring up at the board while she waited for him. "Someone must have taken it then."

Vic muttered a curse.

"What are we going to do?" Aria whispered. She couldn't believe she'd lost their passage off this station.

"I've got a PCSD," Vic replied, patting the pocket of the vest he wore under his cloak. "It doesn't have the funds the other one had … but I might be able to wrangle a deal of some kind."

Aria frowned. "What kind of deal?"

Vic gestured to the terrace of the eatery behind her. "Let me worry about that. Wait here … I'll be back in a bit."

Aria swallowed another question. She still felt sick at losing all those credits—and she couldn't see how he'd manage to get them passage without that PCSD.

Curse the light-fingered piece of shit who'd stolen it. The device was only accessible via thumb-imprint, but a clever thief would eventually be able to find a way in.

"See you later then." She tried to smile, yet failed. She wanted to wish him luck too but refrained from doing so. If she hadn't lost the device, his task would be a lot simpler.

Their gazes met and held before Vic nodded. An instant later, he turned and made his way across the hub toward the doors leading out into the hangars.

Sucking in a slow, deep breath, in an effort to loosen the knots in her stomach, Aria walked onto the eatery's terrace and settled herself at a table from which she had a clear sight of the hub. She picked up a menu and was studying it when a droid floated over.

"Good day," it chirped. "Are you ready to order?"

Vic strode through the wide starkly-white passageway that led past the various docking and cargo bays. It was important to look as if you knew where you were going, and not to loiter. A man who seemed to have a clear destination in mind wasn't nearly as suspicious as one who appeared lost.

As he walked, he tried to come up with a plan. His PCSD only held three thousand hard credits. A hollow sensation settled in the pit of his gut then. That sum wasn't going to get them far.

The droids that wheeled or floated past Vic ignored him, as did the sentients—pilots, technicians, and cargo crew mostly. Luckily, there were plenty of cloaked and hooded figures throughout the space station.

Along the way, Vic passed a banner upon the wall. It was one he'd seen many times when he'd lived here— one that displayed the emblems and mottos of the clans that had allied themselves to the Mir-Ferrins.

Vic's gaze slid down to the third row, to the Mir-Riorde clan insignia, a black moon. Underneath was their motto: *Fidelity and Fortitude.*

His mouth thinned. Those words summed up his family. His father and his uncle had lived to serve the Mir-Ferrins, no matter the cost, as had Vic once. His father and uncle had both died in the line of duty, and Vic was now a cyborg. The price had been too high.

The metal floor beneath his feet started to vibrate then, and Vic looked away from the banner to see a squad of black and bronze armored figures appear at the end of the passageway.

His pulse started to race.

It had been a while since he'd been in close quarters with other cyborgs; since his desertion, Vic had made a point of avoiding military hubs.

As such, the sight of his brethren came as a shock.

They walked as one, boots stomping in unison on the metal floor, arms pumping at their sides. Their faces were blank, the silver rims of their eye plants gleaming in the harsh overhead lighting.

There was nowhere to go. Vic could have ducked into the cargo bay he'd just passed, but it would look suspicious. He was going to have to keep walking.

Armor rattling, they approached him.

Vic shifted closer to the wall and kept moving.

He walked by them, forcing himself not to avert his gaze.

Even so, their blank, soulless eyes chilled him.

He'd come close to being one of them.

Some of the cyborgs surveyed him as they passed—taking in his cloaked form, hooded face, and the duffel bag he carried slung over his shoulder. They were a surveillance squad patrolling Omega's deck.

Vic tensed, readying himself to be surrounded and questioned. If they asked for his ID, he was in trouble; a visiting bioengineer had no reason to be down here. But, to his relief, the patrol didn't break their stride. Perhaps they'd been sent elsewhere, for they marched by him and continued up the corridor.

Slowly letting out the breath he hadn't even realized he'd been holding, Vic continued on his way.

Reaching a large private landing bay, he stepped through the doors and halted.

He'd chosen this bay on purpose. It was the one he'd escaped from over six years earlier. He'd gotten lucky that day; the pilot had been loading cargo into the hold but had left his freighter's main hatch open. Vic and Obsidian had slipped inside and hidden in the bathroom.

By the time the pilot discovered he had a stowaway, they'd been far from Platinum 5.

Vic surveyed the line of craft docked in the bay; as he'd expected, most of them were freighters.

Jidea had been on his side when he deserted from Mir-Ferrin space fleet, yet he couldn't rely on good fortune this time around.

Not with Aria's life at risk.

Moving down the walkway that led in front of the freighters, Vic studied each one. Most of the craft were Mir-Ferrin ships, with the same arrowhead shape as *The Wayfarer*.

Vic's stride slowed as he passed one of the ships. A tall reptilian figure was overseeing a service-droid as it refueled the ship. The Rendak pilot turned, watching Vic's approach, flat eyes narrowing.

He kept walking.

Vic had done enough deals with Rendak over the years to know it was wise to choose another pilot. They were too shrewd, mercenary, and ruthless for a situation like this one.

He passed another Mir-Ferrin freighter and caught sight of a human couple arguing just inside the hatch. Breaking off their insults, they glanced his way, gazes settling upon the cloaked figure approaching.

Vic stifled a sigh. He didn't care for the calculating glint in the woman's eye or the nakedly suspicious look on the man's face. No, that ship wouldn't do either.

Halfway down the walkway, he caught sight of a shabby, lozenge-shaped cargo ship. The shape was distinctive; it was a Mir-Lelith freighter.

On the rusted hull, the faded name—*CS Vertigo*—was visible.

Vic slowed his pace.

The ship was in poor condition, but Mir-Lelith was a good choice. He didn't want to employ a Mir-Ferrin pilot; it was too risky.

Someone was working on the freighter's hull, welding mask in place. Sparks sprayed out from the ship's belly.

Vic approached, waving to attract the individual's attention.

They ceased work, switched off the welding machine, and stepped back, pushing up their visor.

A female, human face frowned up at him. "What?"

Vic wished he was able to flash the woman a smile. "I'm looking for someone to take me … and a companion … to Cadex 12 in ten hours' time. Are you available?"

The woman pulled a face. "That's a bit short notice."

It was, but Vic and Aria had worked it out.

They still had a few hours until the virology laboratory shut down for the day. They'd wait until the lab had been closed for an hour. The pair of them would make sure all the lab techs had left before Aria went in. She'd need around half an hour to destroy all the samples of the bacteria before exiting. After that, they'd meet at the rendezvous point and make their way down from Delta to Omega before taking a walkway here.

It was a journey that would take another hour—as this station was huge. Ten hours gave them a bit of flexibility if they got delayed for any reason.

"No questions asked," Vic replied.

The woman muttered something under her breath and ducked out from under the hull of her ship. Straightening up, she took off her heavy welding gloves, regarding Vic speculatively. Her gaze lingered on his eye plant.

Curiosity lit in her grey eyes before her lips pursed. "I don't usually take passengers," she said after a pause. "They often bring trouble."

Vic wasn't going to argue with her there. He knew from experience just how true that was. However, he was in the same line of business as this woman and knew what would motivate her.

"I can make it worth your while," he said after a pause.

"You'd better," she replied, pulling off her mask. Dark-blonde curls sprang free. The woman appeared to be in her early thirties. She wore a shrewd expression. "Twenty thousand credits up front."

Vic stilled. The price was extortionate, and he didn't have it. However, as he'd entered the landing bay, he'd come up with an idea.

His gaze traveled past the pilot's shoulder, and he ran a speculative, and critical, eye over the battered exterior of the cargo ship. The *CS Vertigo* was a rust bucket. "Looks like your ship has seen better days," he murmured. "Are you sure it's even spaceworthy?"

"She's sound," the woman replied, her tone sharpening. Nonetheless, the tightening of her features let him know he'd hit a nerve. "Are you willing to pay twenty thousand credits or not?"

"No," he replied quietly. "I can offer you something much better."

# 23. I'M GLAD YOU'RE WITH ME

ARIA WAS SIPPING a cup of tea when she spotted Vic moving toward her through the crowd.

Relief barreled into her, and she lowered her cup, exhaling sharply.

He made his way onto the terrace and pulled out a chair opposite her.

Aria met his gaze. "Is it done?"

He nodded.

Aria's breathing quickened, and she leaned forward, lowering her voice to a whisper. "How?"

Vic's mouth twitched. "I've got us passage out of here in ten hours."

Aria's gaze snapped wide, and she opened her mouth to question him further.

Vic reached out, placing a hand over hers. "Not now."

"What would you like?" The utility-droid had appeared from nowhere and hovered at Vic's elbow. "A glass of house ale," Vic replied, "and a large plate of fridolas."

"Of course … right away." The droid floated off.

Aria cocked an eyebrow. "Fridolas?"

"They're a specialty on Platinum 5 … deep-fried parcels filled with meat and cheese."

"Sounds delicious." Aria pulled a face then. "Although I don't know how you can eat right now."

"I'm starving, and the food on this station is some of the best in the sector." His gaze went to her nearly finished cup of tea. "You haven't eaten, I take it?"

She shook her head. "My stomach has closed." Aria cast a furtive look over her shoulder then, to make sure the droid hadn't glided up behind her again. The eatery's terrace wasn't busy at this hour; they had privacy. "So … who's giving us passage?"

"A pilot named Greta Mir-Hamil ... she owns a Mir-Lelith freighter and has agreed to take us to Cadex 12."

Aria's breathing caught. "How in the Gods did you—"

"I'll explain everything later," Vic cut her off smoothly, holding her gaze. "But rest assured, Greta will be waiting for us."

Aria regarded him warily. "How did you pay for the passage?"

He held her gaze. "I gave her a deposit of two thousand credits ... and she's agreed to accept the rest once we reach Cadex 12. Lady Jenna will be happy to oblige."

"She accepted such a small deposit?"

Vic nodded. "The woman's desperate."

Aria frowned. What did he mean by that?

A large platter of deep-fried parcels arrived then, along with a tall, chilled glass of ale for Vic.

The aroma of rich meat drifted across the table, and despite her earlier assertion, Aria's stomach rumbled.

Vic's mouth twitched. "I thought you said you weren't hungry?"

"I'm not ... that smells good though."

Reaching out, Vic took a parcel and bit down on it. Then, with a sigh, he settled back in his seat. When he'd swallowed his mouthful, he spoke once more. "We'll need to stow our bags. I spotted lockers in the corridor outside the loading bay we're leaving from ... they'll do," he said, reaching for his ale.

Aria nodded. Neither of them needed to be encumbered with luggage in the coming hours.

"We'll also need to do some shopping," he added.

"For a laser-pistol?"

Back on the passenger liner, they'd discussed Vic buying a weapon. He'd deliberately not brought one with him from Cadex 12, as he didn't want Platinum 5's spaceport security asking him too many difficult questions.

Vic popped another parcel into his mouth, chewing slowly before he washed it down with a gulp of ale. He then leaned forward. "I'm also going to try and get hold of a detonator of some kind," he said, lowering his voice to a whisper.

Aria stiffened. "For the lab?"

He nodded.

"Do we have enough credits left?"

"Yes."

Aria exhaled sharply. "You don't think destroying the samples in a vaporizer is enough?"

"No … we need to be sure they can't just go in and make more."

She frowned. "Lady Jenna promised me one of her people will take care of that."

Indeed, the clan-lady had assured her that the same agent who'd procured her pass had also hacked the virology lab's database. As soon as the bacteria were destroyed, they'd delete all related files. Malik had also hinted that their people on the inside would find a way to 'deal with' the scientists and technicians involved in the creation of the Starellusbacter in the aftermath. Aria didn't like to dwell on that. It was ruthless—but then so was creating a biological weapon that could potentially kill millions.

"That might be the case," Vic replied after a brief pause. "But since Lady Jenna wants this done properly, it's up to us to make sure there are no loose ends."

Aria wrapped her fingers around her now cold cup of tea. "Will you be able to get hold of a detonator?" she murmured. "I don't imagine they're easy to find on a station like this."

"They're not." Vic's mouth twitched once more. "Unless you know where to look."

"I have good news, brother."

Elijah looked up from where he was cutting into a rare fillet of steak. "About what?"

Across the vast obsidian table, Lucas's face split into a cocky grin. "Varis and his team have made a breakthrough."

Elijah stilled, the fine hair on the back of his neck prickling. "I thought they were some way off discovering a cure?"

Lucas met his eye. His bright smile tightened then. He hadn't been pleased to discover his elder brother had been poking around in the virology lab.

Elijah didn't care though. He was clan-lord—no corner of this station was off-limits to him. He'd go where he wanted and ask whatever he wished of anyone.

The brothers sat in the clan-lord's informal dining chamber—a room decorated in soft bronze. A huge floor-to-ceiling window of tempered glass looked out on the glowing sphere of Formidian.

Lucas's smile remained fixed as he reached for his glass of wine. "It seemed a solution was eluding them, but Varis has been working around the clock … he's currently testing out a new antibiotic, and it appears to be working."

"Surely, rigorous testing needs to be done before we can be certain?" Elijah replied, putting down his cutlery and taking a sip from his glass. "I won't put our own people in danger unless I'm certain the antibiotic is a failsafe cure."

Lucas snorted before making a dismissive gesture with his hand. "There's no such thing as 'failsafe', brother."

"There has to be," Elijah replied, his tone hardening, "when it comes to the Starellusbacter. You're not one of the Gods, Lucas … you're not infallible, and neither are your plans."

Lucas heaved a long-suffering sigh and took a large gulp of wine. He then put his glass down with a 'click' on the polished surface between them. "Sometimes I think you lack the stomach to be clan-lord, Eli," he said mildly.

Elijah sat back in his chair and surveyed Lucas. "Why is that? Because I put the brakes on you? Someone has to, Lucas. You've created a beast … and you need to know how to control it before you let it out of its cage."

"I know that." Lucas picked up his knife and fork then and attacked his steak, eating with neat, deft movements.

Elijah watched him a moment before he, too, resumed eating.

Few things seemed to ruffle Lucas. However, of late, Elijah had come to suspect his brother's unflappable attitude and easy smiles were merely a ruse. He wasn't as easygoing as he seemed.

"Anyway," Lucas said finally, as he speared a juicy piece of steak with his fork, "We're making significant progress. Varis assures me the testing will take another week at most … then we'll be ready." His dark gaze glinted as he flashed Elijah another toothy grin. "I suggest we go in hard. We should strike Staturine II first."

Aria shifted her weight from one foot to the other, her gaze traveling around the machinery warehouse. The eerie quiet in here made her jumpy.

This space wasn't at all like the hub she'd waited in earlier. Although the walls were starkly white, this area wasn't brightly lit. The warehouse was a shadowy, cavernous space with dull-grey girders stretching overhead. The air smelled of engine grease. There weren't any Mir-Ferrin banners in here, no tinkling music playing, just large containers ready to be shipped across the sector.

Vic had stepped inside one of the containers earlier, disappearing behind a rubber curtain—and hadn't yet reappeared.

She was starting to worry.

Vic had assured her this was the place to buy weapons on the station if you wanted to avoid the eye of the authorities.

It didn't surprise Aria that he knew about it; nonetheless, the long wait made her question his decision to come here.

She shivered then, pulling her robes tighter about her. They didn't waste heating on the warehouses.

Aria cast yet another glance at the entrance to the container and considered whether she should go inside and see what had happened to Vic. Indeed, she'd just taken a step toward it when he appeared.

Her gaze roamed over him. "Success?"

He nodded, taking her arm, and guiding her toward the bronze doors on the far side of the warehouse. He then drew back his cloak, to show her the laser-pistol holster around his hip.

"And the detonator?"

"Got it." He patted a pocket on the thigh of his cargos, which showed a rectangular outline. "It's a mining charge … crude but effective."

Aria nodded. She hadn't thought he'd manage to get a pyro-detonator—for those were expensive and hard to find, and Vic was short on time and nearly out of credits. "That'll do."

They exited the warehouse and took a network of deserted white tunnels to the nearest walkway. This one would take them back to the central stem.

Upon the walkway, they halted, letting it carry them toward their destination.

There was no hurry; they still had a couple of hours until Aria had to make her move.

Nonetheless, Aria was restless. Her chest constricted then, her belly fluttering, and she tightened her grip on the handrail that led around the walkway. Although she'd been cold inside that warehouse, she was now sweating under her Ardex mask and heavy robes.

*I can't mess this up.*

Vic had done well. He'd found them passage off Platinum 5 and procured a pistol and a detonator. They were ready to go now, but nerves were kicking in. Lady Jenna had charged her with this task, and she couldn't let her down.

"Breathe." Vic stepped up behind her, one hand wrapping around her arm.

Aria moved into him, bracing herself against his strength and exhaling sharply. She hadn't realized she'd been breathing shallowly and holding on to each breath as if scared to release it. "Yes … I need to remember to do that."

"You do … it's difficult to think straight with a lack of oxygen."

She huffed a nervous laugh. "Really?"

"Really."

Aria sucked in a large lungful of air before releasing it slowly. She then leaned into the hard warmth of his body, and her tension eased, just a little.

"I'm glad you're with me, Vic," she whispered.

"So am I," he murmured back.

# 24. TIME TO GO

ELIJAH ROLLED OVER onto his back, staring up at the shadowy ceiling of his bedchamber.

He'd gone to bed a couple of hours earlier, but he was still wide awake.

Swearing, he pushed aside the covers and rose to his feet. Padding across the cool, polished floor of his chamber, he went to the window and looked out across the star-strewn curtain of space.

Usually, the sight put Elijah at ease, but tonight, he couldn't relax.

He hadn't been able to do so in days.

Not since Aria had run out on him.

Not since Lucas pushed ahead with his project.

And certainly not since he'd learned Doctor Varis was almost ready to hand over the antidote for the Starellusbacter. Surely it couldn't be ready yet. Wouldn't they have to make a huge quantity of antidote first?

Dragging a hand through his hair, Elijah cursed again, vehemently this time.

There was no getting around it. His conscience was bothering him.

Elijah's mouth twisted. He wasn't his father; that was for certain. Mican Mir-Ferrin had readily agreed to Lucas's project, had been keen to push forward with it.

But Elijah had never shared their enthusiasm.

A couple of years earlier, he'd dismissed it as impossible, but he couldn't do so any longer.

They were on the brink now, close to releasing the bacteria on their enemies. Lucas already had a plan on how to do it—during dinner, he'd explained with enthusiasm how easy it would be to have a droid set the Starellusbacter free on a passenger liner bound for Staturine II. They'd time it so that the bacteria circulated shortly before arrival—that way those infected wouldn't sicken until after they'd disembarked. After they'd unknowingly spread the bacteria through Briscay's spaceport.

Sure, they'd likely kill more than just Mir-Brennans, but no Mir-Ferrins would be traveling to that planet, so their own people would be safe.

And once they did, there would be no going back.

Elijah leaned forward, bracing his palms on the glass. It was cold against his skin, yet he welcomed the chill.

It helped him focus his thoughts.

All diplomatic relations had been severed between their clans these days. Jenna Mir-Brennan's strong leadership concerned Elijah. He knew she was planning to take back Idral. He still had agents on the inside, and one of them was an administrator at Castle Valnor on Staturine II. His spy fed him regular intelligence. The clan-lady was rebuilding her space fleet rapidly and had commissioned the fabrication of arms. She was readying herself for conflict.

And if he used their bioweapon, she'd never get the chance.

Elijah inhaled deeply, pushing harder against the tempered glass.

He was a Mir-Ferrin. He wanted to get the upper hand over his enemies. He wanted control of the Rith sector, to have the other clans bow before him.

But not like this.

Some paths led to destruction, and Elijah's gut told him this was one.

He was the only one who could stop this, and he had a choice to make.

Pushing himself off the window, Elijah retrieved his clothes from where he'd thrown them over the back of the chair. Then he started to get dressed.

"I'll wait for you here."

Aria tore her gaze from watching white and bronze jumpsuit-clad figures flow in and out of the elevators leading into the station's central stem and focused on the cloaked figure standing next to her. Meeting Vic's eye, she nodded.

It was a good meeting spot, and as close as they could get to the virology lab without Vic drawing too much attention to himself

This hub was the main thoroughfare on Delta deck, providing passage through to the central stem elevators. Several moving walkways led off the space, like the spokes of a wheel. Above, another glass dome, like the one in the arrivals terminal, let in a view of glittering stars against a swathe of inky black. The starry roof dulled the ever-present, icy brightness, making this place a pleasant spot to wait.

Aria had been worried they'd get in trouble for loitering here—but a few bars and restaurants lined the area. The restaurants were closed at this hour, while the bars were busy and rowdy. Aria and Vic had chosen a standing table on the terrace, where they'd been nursing drinks for the past hour.

Around them, marines and pilots drank heavily; raucous laughter and aggressive banter boomed against the background of a deep, steady bass, ringing across the hub.

Aria cleared her throat, glancing back at the walkway entrance on the far side of the brightly lit space. "That's the last of them then?"

"Yes," Vic replied. He'd been checking off each of the lab techs as they emerged from the walkway over the last hour, ticking them off the list of those who'd been working the last shift. "They've all gone home … we're ready to move."

Aria dragged in a deep breath, her skin prickling.

Finally, the waiting was over. The anticipation had been tying her up in knots.

"I'm giving you forty minutes," Vic informed her then, moving close. Around them, the bar was so rowdy no one could overhear their conversation. Nonetheless, they were both being careful. "After that, I'll come looking for you." He then reached out and tapped Aria's wrist-comm. "If you get into trouble, punch this thing."

Aria swallowed. "I will." In addition to the encrypted, voice-activated channel he'd set up, Vic had added a secondary emergency signal. If she was in trouble, and couldn't talk, all she had to do was tap the screen four times in rapid succession and it would alert Vic that she was in danger.

Of course, he couldn't reach her inside the virology lab—but knowing she could alert him if things went awry steadied her nerves, just a little.

Aria pushed herself away from the table. "See you soon," she said lightly.

She couldn't delay this any longer. It was time to go.

"Hey, gorgeous," one of the drunken marines slurred as Aria moved away from the table. He was a male Nandoon, and Aria had seen him glance her way a few times over the past hour. However, she'd been careful to avoid his eye.

The marine lurched toward her now, wattles swinging, but Aria ducked her gaze and shifted away. She really didn't need to be accosted by an amorous Nandoon right now.

Without a backward glance, she struck out across the hub, weaving her way through the flow of citizens coming and going from the walkways and elevators. Despite that it was now the middle of the night on Platinum 5, the station was as busy as ever.

As she walked, Aria felt Vic's gaze on her, the heat of it between her shoulder blades.

Her pulse quickened. He couldn't assist her any longer; the rest was up to her.

It was a relief to step onto the moving walkway, to be whisked along. Yet the tinny music just stretched her nerves even tauter. There were two walkways in this smooth-sided tunnel, each going in different directions. A gleaming strip of white—a center console—divided the walkways.

Reaching down, Aria placed a hand over the small purse she carried across her front.

It contained her keycard and the mining charge. After being pick-pocketed earlier, she'd checked her bag numerous times over the past couple of hours. She couldn't misplace either of those items.

Reassured, Aria counted the landings she passed, and when she reached the third one, she stepped off the walkway and set off down a stark, narrow passage. Like everywhere else on Platinum 5, it was so white, her eyes smarted. In contrast to the other areas of the station, the sharp smell of disinfectant now filled her nostrils.

The passage reached a dead end. Before her sat a blank metal door with two scanners: one at eye level, the other a few feet below it.

Aria halted before the door and hurriedly drew out her keycard.

Noting her hands were shaking, she clenched her jaw. *Get yourself together.*

She swiped the card across the bottom scanner and received a 'bleep' in response before a tinny voice commanded. "Retinal scan required."

Sucking in a deep breath, Aria leaned forward and placed her right eye in line with the scanner.

She then prayed to every one of the galactic gods.

Varussa Mir-Barus was a real identity: a biologist who'd paid a few visits to this facility in the past. The contact lens Aria wore in her right eye was Varussa's retinal imprint—Aria just hoped Jenna's agent knew what they were doing.

If the scanner didn't recognize her eye, it would set the alarms off.

Seconds passed, and then the scanner bleeped once more. A heavy clunking noise followed as the locks disengaged.

"Access permitted."

Exhaling sharply. Aria pushed her way indoors. *Breathe, remember?*

Inside the laboratory, a host of familiar smells hit her: the sharp tang of chlorine, acetone, sulfur, and antibacterial soap. The lights were dim; the last lab tech to leave had turned them down before leaving, and the air was suffocatingly warm.

Aria walked through the main laboratory, her boots echoing in the stillness. Her spine tingled as she moved, for she knew security cameras would be on her. There was no way to easily shut them off, not even Jenna's spy had that authority, but they'd assured the clan-lady the lab cameras weren't monitored.

In a few hours—after this lab blew up, when they played the recording—they'd see a female Nandoon enter and leave the laboratory. But they wouldn't recognize Aria, and that was what mattered.

Glancing around her—just to ensure the lab was indeed empty, for the deep shadows made her feel as if she wasn't really alone—Aria made her way to the isolation unit. Outside, she donned a protective suit and goggles. She also put on a mask, pulling it down so it only covered her mouth. Her Ardex proboscis was too large to fit inside it, but the appendage already had an air filter inside it anyway.

She entered the room and halted in the center of the tiled floor, getting her bearings. A gleaming bench sat along one wall, with safety hoods above it, while a row of freezers and refrigerators sat opposite. Directly in front of her was a storage unit, while the autoclave and vaporizer were at her back.

Aria stepped forward. She'd already studied the layout of this space and knew where to find most things. It was time to move.

Reaching into her purse, she withdrew the charge. She'd been tempted to leave setting this until last. However, if she ran out of time while destroying the bacteria and had to get out of the lab fast, she didn't want to forget about it.

She adjusted the digital clock carefully—as Vic had shown her earlier—for three hours from now. That would give them enough time to get down to Omega deck, to their ship, and off Platinum 5 before it blew.

Setting the device, and noting that her hands were still shaking, Aria fixed it, out of direct sight, under the bench.

Her heart was now pounding.

This was happening. The mining charge was set. There was no going back.

She had to focus on locating all the sample dishes containing the virus and destroying them. Of course, she'd considered just setting the charge and running, trusting that the explosion would destroy all traces of the bacteria.

But that was too risky. What if the charge didn't blow? Or, worse still, what if the explosion released the Starellusbacter into the air? It could end up infecting the whole space station.

No, she had to vaporize all the samples before leaving.

Aria strode to the storage drawers and began at one end, sorting through the sample dishes. It was a laborious process, and Aria started to sweat. Her snout hung down and kept getting in her line of sight. Clenching her jaw, she brushed it out of the way.

As she'd expected, all the samples were carefully labeled—but it took her a while to find the ones she wanted.

And, finally, there it was—a black spiderweb pattern upon a blood-red culture.

"Starellusbacter," she whispered. The back of her arms prickled, and sweat now trickled down her back.

The Mir-Ferrins were challenging the gods by creating such a weapon, but they didn't care. They'd destroy the Rith Sector if they weren't stopped. Adrenaline surged then, her blood roaring in her ears.

Suddenly, despite that she was afraid, she was glad she'd agreed to do this.

Reaching in with gloved hands, Aria carefully collected a stack of Petri dishes. She then carried them over to the vaporizer. She wouldn't be using the sterilizer to kill these bacteria—instead, she was incinerating them.

She deposited the first batch in the vaporizer, shut the hatch, and punched the start button. The machine started with a whoosh. It would take three minutes to complete the job; meanwhile, Aria would ready the next batch.

Her pulse sped up further then. There were more samples than she'd thought—she'd need to work fast to get this done in forty minutes.

She was bent over the drawer, collecting another stack of dishes, when the 'click' of a door closing behind her made her freeze.

An instant later, her heart leaped into her throat when a rough male voice demanded, "Who the fuck are you?"

# 25. I'M NOT A MONSTER

HARDLY DARING TO breathe, Aria turned.

A tall figure, clad in a protective suit, faced her. For an instant, she thought it was Vic, but even though he wore a mask, she quickly realized it wasn't. Night-black hair fell to the man's shoulders, and even behind the goggles, she recognized his dark eyes.

"Elijah," she gasped before she could help herself.

The clan-lord's gaze bored into her. "Do I know you?"

Aria swallowed hard. *Shit.*

His attention then shifted to the stack of sample dishes she clutched. "What are you doing?"

"Just cleaning up," she replied, striving to keep the panic out of her voice.

"In the middle of the night?"

"Doctor Varis asked me to do this two days ago … but I've been running behind."

Elijah surveyed her, his eyebrows drawing together. "I recognize your voice," he murmured. "I repeat … who are you?"

"Varussa Mir-Barus."

His frown deepened, and he took a step closer to her. "How do you know my name?"

"You're the Mir-Ferrin clan-lord," she replied huskily. "Everyone knows who you are."

"But few people would dare to greet me by my first name." His head tilted. The mask hid his nose and mouth, but she sensed his smile. "That's quite a disguise, Aria … you almost had me fooled."

Vic checked his wrist-comm. Two minutes had passed since he'd last looked.

Fingers clenching around the glass of ale he'd been nursing since Aria's departure, he tried to curb his impatience, his frustration.

Nonetheless, it boiled inside him.

He hated not knowing what was happening, or if Aria was in danger.

It was hard to maintain a casual appearance. He pretended to watch passersby, while his attention kept moving to the farthest walkway, where Aria had disappeared.

Since then, a handful of individuals had taken the same tunnel—which led to the virology lab, and then on to the main research facility.

Only one of them had made him nervous: a cloaked figure. Tall and possibly human, with a hood covering their face, the individual—most likely male, judging from the height—had left the elevators and strode purposefully toward the walkway.

Vic had tracked his passage, a tickle of misgiving feathering down his spine.

He then reminded himself that several cloaked figures were traveling about this station. A few races, the Daksari and the Belnians among them, habitually wore cloaks with deep cowls. It was the reason why Vic didn't attract many glances.

Nonetheless, he liked to see the faces of those taking that walkway. He didn't want one of the technicians returning to the lab without him noticing.

Glancing down at his wrist-comm once again, Vic scowled.

Damn it, it had been twenty minutes. He was ready to climb the walls.

He'd told Aria he'd give her forty minutes, but maybe he needed to wait closer, by the lab entrance. It was risky, as there would be security cameras over the door, but that cloaked figure preyed on his mind.

He had to make sure no one was lurking around, waiting to pounce on Aria when she departed the lab.

Vic was wrestling with the decision of whether to stay or go when someone tapped his shoulder.

He turned to see a huge male Nandoon looming over him.

Vic tensed; he'd spotted the marine earlier. He'd been staring at Aria. "What?" he asked gruffly, knowing that his expressionless face would be off-putting.

"That female you were with earlier," the Nandoon huffed, his dark eyes gleaming with a surfeit of drink. "Is she available?"

Vic inhaled slowly, irritation spiking through him. He didn't have the time or patience for this. But he was also wary of drawing too much attention to himself.

"No," he replied after a pause. "She's with me."

The Nandoon's sloping shoulders tensed, his snout twitching. "That's a rare coupling ... a Nandoon and a human."

Vic shrugged. "Rare but not unheard of."

The Nandoon's gaze narrowed as he surveyed Vic's shadowed face. "What are you ... a cyborg?"

Vic's pulse quickened. "No ... I'm modified." He inclined his head. "My mate likes it ... she's had some mods made of her own."

Wattles quivering with distaste, the marine drew back from him, making it clear he wouldn't be asking about the comely female Nandoon again.

Vic turned back to his drink, his gaze sweeping the crowded hub once more—when his wrist-comm started to vibrate.

Aria's blood roared in her ears. Syr grant her mercy, she was done for.

Sliding her left hand over where her right still gripped the samples, she tapped her wrist-comm's screen four times. There was nothing Vic could do to help her right now, but she had to let him know she was in trouble.

Elijah's gaze never moved from hers. "So, now we've got that out of the way … I'll ask you again. What are you doing?"

Aria drew in a deep breath. Gods, she had to move. However, Elijah stood between her and the vaporizer.

Staring back at him, she decided the truth was her only option. "I'm destroying the Starellusbacter."

Elijah raised his brows. "How do you even know about it?"

"I overheard you and Lucas discussing it in the gardens … on the morning of our wedding. It's why I ran."

A jolt when through Elijah's tall, athletic form. An instant later, understanding glinted in his dark-brown eyes. "You didn't get cold feet then?"

"Not until that point, Elijah," she snapped. "But discovering you and Lucas were hatching a plan to wipe out the Mir-Brennans with a bioweapon killed your appeal." The sarcasm in her voice was raw, yet she didn't care. All she could think about was the timer on that charge, silently ticking down.

His brow furrowed. "The project was Lucas's, not mine."

"Maybe, but you sanctioned it … I heard you."

Silence fell, and although she couldn't see his facial expression, she sensed his discomfort. "You're right, I did," he answered, his voice lowering. "But not any longer."

Aria stilled. Her heart started to hammer against her ribs as realization dawned. "That's why you're down here in the middle of the night?"

"Yes, I couldn't go through with it." He took a step toward her then. "You're quite a woman, Aria," he murmured. "I can't believe you're here … doing this on your own."

Aria sucked in a deep breath. Best he didn't know about Vic, or the fact the Mir-Brennan clan-lady had sent her. "Save your compliments," she growled. "Are you going to stand there yapping or step aside so I can get this done?"

He inclined his head before shifting out of her way and gesturing to the vaporizer behind him. "Go ahead."

Warily, Aria moved past him, opened the vaporizer, and inserted the new batch. Then, starting it, she swiveled to find Elijah had opened the freezer in the corner. "There are samples in here too," he informed her.

"Collect them and bring them over to the vaporizer," she replied. "But be careful."

He nodded before delving into the freezer. Like her, Elijah wore gloves; even so, he handled the dishes gingerly and with obvious distaste.

Feeling a little light-headed, as relief and confusion both vied for dominance, Aria returned to the drawer and cleared it of the last of the Starellusbacter samples.

The vaporizer finished its current cycle, and she filled it once more.

Impatience beat within her as she opened the rest of the drawers, searching for any other Petri dishes containing the super-bacterium—but that appeared the last of the fresh samples. Meanwhile, Elijah had taken out a large stack of frozen ones.

Waiting for the vaporizer to finish its cycle, Aria cut Elijah a sharp look. He'd gone suspiciously silent, and she didn't trust him.

"Don't look at me like that," he said, his voice roughening. "I'm not a monster."

She snorted. "That's debatable."

Their gazes met and held. The eyes were the only part of their faces they could see.

"We used to be friends," Elijah reminded her after a short pause. "I *wanted* to marry you, Aria ... I was actually looking forward to it."

The intimacy in his voice made her pulse stutter. She didn't need reminding of the promise they'd once made each other. She cleared her throat. "Yeah, well, you messed things up, didn't you?"

Silence stretched between them then before the dull whirr and click of the vaporizer finishing its cycle filled the isolation unit. Tearing her attention from Elijah's, Aria filled the vaporizer once more before glancing down at her wrist-comm.

*Thirty minutes.*

Gods, she still had at least five more batches to incinerate. Now that she'd alerted him, Vic would be waiting at the door when she exited.

However, in a bizarre turn of events, the Mir-Ferrin clan-lord was standing a few feet away, masked and gloved up, and helping her dispose of the Starellusbacter.

"This is quite a risk you're taking," Aria said then, wishing she could see his face. "Aren't you afraid you'll get caught?"

Damn it, was she actually worried about him now? The truth was that she and Elijah had once been good friends. She'd trusted him enough to agree to spend the rest of her life with him. That trust had been broken, yet the remnants of the bond they'd once shared were still there, unspoken, between them.

"I'm at the top of the chain of command," he replied, the Mir-Ferrin arrogance surfacing. "If I wished, I could order this entire lab cleared … however, I don't wish to make an enemy of my brother. Lucas and I are the only ones left. That's why I took precautions tonight. I have a security pass that won't reveal my identity … and I disabled the cameras both inside and outside the lab remotely before I came down here."

Aria absorbed this information. It was a relief to know he was cautious. "Lucas is a psychopath," she muttered. "Who cares if you make an enemy of him?"

Elijah snorted a laugh, and Aria clenched her jaw. "All that 'blood is thicker than water' talk is bullshit," she growled, surprised at the depth of the anger that quickened inside her. "No one can hurt you the way family can."

Elijah's eyes widened. "You found the tracking device your father planted on you then?"

Her own gaze narrowed. "Was that your idea?"

"No. I didn't know anything about it … until he contacted me."

Aria scowled. She wasn't sure whether to believe him or not—although it wasn't important.

Right now, the only thing that mattered was destroying the rest of these samples and getting out of this lab.

# 26. A CHANGE OF PLAN

FORTY-FIVE MINUTES after entering the isolation unit, Aria destroyed the last batch of samples.

"Are you sure there aren't any others?" she asked Elijah as he checked the freezer next to the one he'd emptied.

"One of the lab techs assured me that the frozen samples were only in the end freezer," he replied, straightening up. "And it seems he wasn't lying."

Aria huffed out a relieved breath. Her legs suddenly felt rubbery. She couldn't relax yet.

Exiting the isolation unit, they stripped off their protective gear and shoved it down the garbage chute.

Without another word to Elijah, Aria turned and made for the doors.

Jidea, Mistress of Fate, had struck her hammer tonight. For a brief spell, Aria and Elijah had been allies again—but it couldn't last. She needed to distance herself from him. She had to leave.

However, she was two strides from the door, when his hand caught her arm, pulling her up short. "Not so fast."

Aria struggled against him. "Let me go," she hissed between clenched teeth.

"I don't think so." His voice had an edge to it now. "Now that I've found my fiancée, I don't intend to lose her again."

"What?" Aria twisted hard against him, but his grip was like steel. "I ran away, remember? I don't want to marry you."

"We had a misunderstanding, Aria … one that's been cleared up."

"You can't wipe the slate clean," she ground out. "It doesn't work that way."

Elijah steered her toward the door. "Come on … when they discover the Starellusbacter has been destroyed, it'll be chaos. I need to keep you safe. Time to return to Alpha deck."

Panic ignited under Aria's ribs, and she tried again to pull free from his hold. She was a tall, strong woman, but she couldn't shake him off. "No," she gasped. "Let me go."

"I can't do that."

"You can't *make* me marry you!"

Elijah barked a bitter laugh. "You really do have a poor opinion of me … don't you?"

Reaching out, he punched a gloved hand against the door panel. He then maneuvered her ahead of him out into the passageway beyond.

Aria knew Vic would be there—and he was.

He'd flattened himself up against the wall next to the door, and when it slid open, and Aria and Elijah emerged, he pounced.

A blow to the side of the head sent Elijah reeling sideways. He released his grip on Aria just enough for her to wrench herself free. She threw herself forward, colliding with the wall opposite.

She turned to see Vic towering over Elijah, laser-pistol aimed at his head.

The clan-lord's hood had fallen back, and he was staring up at his attacker.

"Elijah Mir-Ferrin," Vic murmured. His voice was as emotionless as his face, yet Aria could feel the fury that vibrated off him. "I can't believe my luck."

Elijah didn't reply. Nonetheless, his dark eyes were defiant, angry, as they flicked from Vic to Aria.

Vic's finger started to squeeze the trigger.

Panic flared under Aria's breastbone as she pushed herself up off the wall. "Don't kill him."

Vic cast her a sharp look. "Why not? He hunted you. He's planning to unleash a biological weapon that could wipe out half this sector. I'd be doing the galaxy a favor."

"He helped me get rid of the bacteria." Vic's eye widened at this news, yet Aria plowed on. "We've done what we came for ... I don't want his blood on your hands."

"I don't care about that."

"Well, I do."

Vic and Aria stared at each other a long moment before she stepped close, her hand closing over his arm. "The job's done ... come on, all of us need to get away from here. We'll ditch him downstairs."

"You won't get away with this," Elijah snarled. "I'll—"

Vic struck out with a booted foot, catching the clan-lord in the ribs.

Elijah's sharp gasp echoed through the corridor.

"One more word and I'll blow a hole in your skull." Vic bit out the words before glancing Aria's way once more. "I really should kill him."

"No." Heart pounding, Aria glanced around her. Damn it, they had to go. Now.

Earlier, she'd thought Elijah was on her side; however, he'd only cooperated with her while it suited him. She was furious at his high-handed manner afterward. Elijah was no longer the gangly teenager she'd roamed Alpha deck with, no longer her friend, but she couldn't let Vic shoot him in the head.

Her lover wasn't thinking straight.

"Get him to his feet," she said curtly. "We don't have time for this."

Vic's jaw tightened, but he complied, hauling Elijah up and jamming the butt of his laser-pistol into the small of his back.

"Pull up your hood," Aria ordered Elijah, as they moved off down the corridor. "And do exactly as we tell you ... I might have an aversion to killing you, but my friend doesn't."

Jaw clenched, the clan-lord obeyed.

Aria moved in close then, walking at Vic's side. Reaching out, she drew the edge of his cloak over his hand, covering the pistol. Now it looked as if they were three companions walking close together, although the ruse wouldn't hold up to close inspection.

Leaving the virology lab behind, they retraced their steps back to the moving walkway. Stepping onto it, they crossed the center console and took the one traveling back toward the central stem hub.

All the while, none of them spoke.

Aria kept casting Vic glances. He'd pulled his hood low over his face, and she was standing on his right side, so she couldn't see his left eye—the only part of his face that revealed his emotions.

Even so, tension hummed off him, as did anger.

He was trying to protect her, yet his feelings for her were clouding his judgment.

As the walkway carried them the last few yards toward the hub, Vic eventually broke the brittle silence. "I'll warn you just once, Mir-Ferrin … one word, one side-ways look, and I'll kill you."

Elijah's shoulders tensed, yet he didn't answer.

That was probably wise.

Aria didn't doubt Vic in the slightest, and she sensed Elijah didn't either.

Entering the central stem hub, they headed toward the bank of elevators. It was getting very late now, and the stream of workers moving across the wide space had lessened. All the shops lining the edge of the hub were closed, save for two rowdy bars. A low thudding bass pulsed across the cavernous space.

Aria fought the urge to scan their surroundings nervously. The thinning crowds made them stick out.

Thankfully, they didn't have to wait long for an elevator—one arrived seconds after Aria called it. Stepping into it, she was relieved to see that it was empty except for a utility-droid with a large trolley of canisters.

The journey down from Delta to Omega deck was silent, although Aria was sure both men and the droid must be able to hear the thundering of her heart.

This wasn't the way their escape was supposed to go.

How were they going to rid themselves of Elijah without attracting unwelcome attention? And where were they going to put him?

She wanted to ask Vic, yet his grim manner dissuaded her, and he didn't break his stride as they left the elevators and got on the walkway.

They kept walking, once on it, heading past the spaceport, the arrivals and departures terminals, and making their way toward the private docking and cargo bays.

And the nearer they got to their destination, the more anxious Aria became. She was sweating heavily under her mask, wig, and heavy robes. Her disguise was truly starting to suffocate her now, and she couldn't wait to rip it off. However, their current predicament held most of her attention.

She kept glancing over her shoulder—half-expecting to see battle-droids storming up the tunnel behind them. Eventually, she leaned close to Vic. "Any ideas for where we should leave him down here?"

Vic cast her a sidelong look. "We'll take him to the ship."

Alarm jolted through her chest. "Is that smart?"

"Don't worry … I have a plan." He paused then before whispering, "Did you set the charge?"

Aria's gaze flicked to where Elijah marched in front of them, shoulders set. She then flashed Vic a tight smile and nodded.

The *CS Vertigo* sat on its landing pad, hatch down, waiting for them.

And despite that he'd made its captain an offer she couldn't refuse, Vic let out a slow, relieved exhale. They'd made it down here without mishap, stopping to pick up their luggage on the way. Aria towed her suitcase behind her and carried his duffel bag over her shoulder.

Things hadn't gone as planned upstairs though—and they didn't need anything else to go wrong.

As they approached the cargo ship, Aria muttered an oath under her breath. "We're leaving in *that*?"

"It's spaceworthy," he replied. "Just."

In truth, the freighter was in bad shape. It looked even shabbier than it had hours earlier. However, it only had to get them to Cadex 12, and no further.

At this hour, the landing bay was deserted. Nonetheless, Vic surveyed the line of freighters parked before them intently. The quiet put his nerves on edge. At the same time, the emptiness aided them. They didn't need pilots and crew hanging around, watching them. Especially, if his idea was going to work.

Their boots echoed through the landing bay, ringing on metal. Vic nudged the clan-lord in the small of his back with his pistol, angling him toward the cargo ship.

He ground his teeth then. Gods help him, he'd wanted to kill Mir-Ferrin. He'd throttled his anger, choked on it, all the way down from the virology lab.

He couldn't understand why Aria wanted to save his life. He remembered her telling him they'd once been friends—but surely, she didn't still have feelings for this piece of shit?

The clan-lord might have helped her destroy the Starellusbacter—although Vic couldn't get his head around that at present—but he'd allowed his scientists to develop it in the first place. He'd also sent battle-droids after Aria, stalking her across the sector.

But since Aria wasn't going to let him kill Elijah Mir-Ferrin, he needed to find another way to deal with him. It had crossed Vic's mind that he could abduct the clan-lord and hand him over to Lady Jenna as a political hostage—however, that would only put Lucas in charge of the Mir-Ferrin clan.

Not a great idea.

No, the clan-lord wasn't coming with them.

They clattered up the ramp and turned right into a narrow passageway. Greta emerged from the cockpit to greet them as they entered the cabin. A small, furry

Gibbit trailed behind her, its dark eyes gleaming as it surveyed their passengers.

However, the moment Greta spied three, rather than two, passengers, she halted, her grey eyes narrowing. The pilot then folded her arms across her chest. "What's this?"

Vic kept his pistol trained on Elijah. "Don't worry, he's not traveling with us." He met Greta's eye then. "Do you have any duct or insulation tape?"

She nodded, her gaze wary.

"Can you fetch it … and hand it to my friend here." Vic nodded to Aria.

Greta opened her mouth as if to argue with him before she snapped it closed once more. Muttering a curse under her breath, she stomped past him and started digging through a storage locker at the back of the cabin. Retrieving a roll of insulation tape, she handed it to Aria, observing the Nandoon with interest. Her attention then shifted back to the prisoner. "You look familiar."

Elijah snorted. The clan-lord's gaze then shifted between Vic and Aria—and Vic didn't care for the look on the man's face.

Clearly, he'd guessed the relationship between them.

Vic nodded to Aria. "Bind his wrists first … behind his back."

She moved to do as bid. However, she'd just started her task when Greta gasped. "Raul's balls … you're the clan-lord."

Beside her, the Gibbit's eyes widened before it gave a strangled cry. "Mir-Ferrin!"

"That's right," Elijah ground out between clenched teeth.

Panic rippled across Greta's round face, her gaze flicking between Vic and Aria. "You'll get me arrested."

"This will get you worse than that," Elijah growled, seizing his opportunity. "If you help them, you and your furry friend here will end up before a firing squad … I'll see to it."

"Tape up his mouth," Vic ordered.

"You're aiding criminals," Elijah continued calmly. "And I'll—"

The rest of his threat cut off as Aria placed a piece of tape across his mouth.

Vic gave a satisfied grunt. "That's better."

# 27. FAR BEHIND

GRETA MIR-HAMIL'S EYES were now the size of moons, and a faint sheen of sweat gleamed on her forehead. "I didn't sign up for this."

Vic held her gaze. "No questions asked, remember?" He took hold of Elijah's arm, but the clan-lord started to struggle.

A punch to the stomach stilled him. Eyes wide and burning with fury, Elijah bent double, his chest heaving.

Vic holstered his pistol and nodded to Greta. "Come on … I need your help." He then took the roll of insulation tape from Aria and handed it to the pilot. "You'll need this."

Greta glanced Aria's way. "And your friend?"

"She's staying here."

In truth, he didn't trust the captain of the *CS Vertigo* not to panic and take off without them. The woman was desperate for the payment he'd offered, but fear might override greed. That was why he was leaving Aria onboard while he and Greta dealt with the clan-lord.

Greta must have realized this as well, for her mouth thinned into a hard line.

"Bring your toolbox too," Vic added. He then turned to Aria. "We'll be right back."

Aria nodded, while Greta turned to the Gibbit. "Keep an eye on things in here," she muttered.

"Yes, Captain," the Gibbit chattered, its bright eyes darting from Greta to the Nandoon.

Vic led the way off the cargo ship, with Greta following close behind carrying her toolbox. Outside, he scanned his surroundings once more, checking to make sure the landing bay was as quiet as earlier.

It was.

He pulled up Elijah's hood, shadowing his face and the line of tape across his mouth, before hauling him up the ramp onto the walkway that led between the docked ships.

Vic then pushed Elijah left toward the far end of the landing bay.

There were lockers there—much bigger than the luggage cabinets where they'd stowed their bags—used for storing machinery parts and cargo.

Drawing up, Vic glanced over at Greta. "Open one of them."

Scowling, she grabbed a screwdriver from her toolbox and pried open the locker nearest. The metal gave way with a groan, the sound echoing obscenely in the quiet landing bay.

Vic glanced around. They had to move fast before someone saw them.

Throwing the door open, he shoved Elijah inside the unlit space. This locker was empty, although it smelled of engine grease and the ozone scent of Crillon residue. Grabbing the roll of tape, Vic knelt and deftly wrapped it around Elijah's ankles.

Once he was done, Vic looked up. His gaze fused for a moment with the clan-lord's—silent understanding passing between them.

If ever they saw each other again, blood would be spilled.

Vic had to give the clan-lord some credit. The man wasn't a coward. He glared at Vic as if he wanted to rip his head off. It wasn't going to help him though.

Vic stared Elijah down, resentment stirring in his gut. This man still thought he had some claim on Aria, but he didn't. "If I hear a squeak out of you before we leave, I'll be only happy to come back here and finish what I started earlier," he growled. "Don't test me, Mir-Ferrin. Aria might have a soft heart, but I don't."

He then slammed the locker shut and nodded to Greta. "Shut it tight."

"Right." She dug around in her toolbox, producing a silver tube of glue. "This should do it." She opened the door a crack to apply a line of clear gel. She then closed it once more and leaned her weight against the door. "It takes a couple of minutes to set."

Vic huffed an impatient sigh. The clock was ticking down. Aria had set the mining charge in the lab—and this door wouldn't hold the clan-lord for very long.

Despite Vic's threat, he'd start kicking at it as soon as they left. Soon this bay would be busy again, and someone would hear him.

They had to go.


Vic strode through the cabin and threw himself onto one of the passenger seats. "Right, let's get out of here."

"You were the one holding us up," Greta grumbled as she stepped up into the cockpit.

Wordlessly, Aria sank down into her seat and clipped on her harness.

Ahead, Greta and her co-pilot were busy flicking switches and turning dials.

A moment later, the engines coughed into life.

Aria tensed, casting another glance Vic's way. Those engines didn't sound in good shape at all. *The Wayfarer* purred compared to this ship. However, his attention was fixed upon the cockpit, where Greta had just switched on the comm console.

"Tower, this is the *CS Vertigo*. We're ready for our 0100 slot. Do we have clearance for takeoff?"

The comm hissed for a moment before a female voice answered. "Affirmative, *CS Vertigo* … you're cleared for departure."

"Thank you."

Moments later, the cargo ship rose off the landing pad, shuddering as the engines increased in pitch.

Aria sucked in a deep breath. She hoped Vic hadn't agreed to pay this woman too much.

The ship rotated then, facing the yawning hangar door. Beyond, the dark curtain of space beckoned.

Aria's pulse quickened, and she closed her eyes, praying fervently to Jidea, Goddess of Fortune, to allow them to leave Platinum 5 without further incident.

When she opened her eyes, the freighter was out of the landing bay and accelerating away from the station. However, Aria remained on tenterhooks. They could still be locked in a tractor beam and hauled back inside.

Her gaze rested on Greta's curly head, watching as the pilot bent over the instrument panel, no doubt charting a course to Cadex 12. Next to her, the Gibbit's small and nimble hands moved fluidly across the controls.

"How long until we make the jump?" Vic asked, anticipating Aria's own question.

"Just another minute," Greta snapped. "I'm locating the nearest lane now."

Endless seconds passed, while anxiety wreathed up inside Aria, making it feel as if a weight sat on her chest—and then *CS Vertigo* lurched forward into hyperspace, leaving Platinum 5 far behind.


Aria collapsed against the back of her seat, her limbs suddenly boneless.

Giddy relief swept through her. Glancing over at Vic, she smiled. "We did it."

Vic looked her way, and his mouth twitched. "We did."

Aria's attention flicked back at the cockpit. Greta was making a show of checking the instruments, but she was sure the woman's ears were flapping. It was best they didn't discuss what they'd done in detail right now.

Meanwhile, Vic looked away, fixing his gaze on the rusting panels overhead.

Studying him, Aria's smile slowly faded. She cleared her throat, drawing his attention once more, "What's wrong … are you angry?"

"No," he replied quietly, shifting his attention back to her. "Not with you, anyway."

She held his gaze. "Do you still resent Lady Jenna … for sending me here?"

He shook his head. "Not any longer. She didn't put a gun to your head … in the end, this was your choice. No, it's Mir-Ferrin. I wanted to kill him," he admitted.

"It wouldn't have changed anything," she said softly.

They continued to stare at each other for a few more moments before Vic replied. "I know."

Aria peeled off the mask then, sighing in relief as the cool air inside the cabin feathered across her itchy, overheated skin.

Gods, that was better.

She removed her wig and gloves too, running her fingers through her sweat-damp hair.

"You're human."

She glanced up to find Greta observing her. Small, with a curvaceous, compact frame, and a wild mane of dark-blonde hair, their pilot had the air of a survivor. She wore grey cargos, heavy boots, and a black shirt—the same style that Vic wore aboard *The Wayfarer*.

Greta's smoke-grey eyes were wide at the sight of her transformation. "Raul's balls," she muttered. "Not more surprises."

Aria flashed her a smile. "This is the last one, I promise."

"Greta, meet Aria," Vic introduced them.

The pilot's mouth pursed before she gestured to her copilot. "This is Frol, my first-mate." Her gaze narrowed then. "Are you going to tell me what you're up to?"

Aria tensed. "I think it's safer for you if you don't know."

"It is," Vic agreed.

Greta folded her arms across her chest. "That was before you dragged the Mir-Ferrin clan-lord onto my ship. I'll never be able to go back to Platinum 5 now, thanks to you two."

"There are plenty of other places to trade in the sector," Vic replied.

A nerve ticked in Greta's cheek. "I knew I shouldn't have accepted this job," she muttered. "That's what happens when you get greedy."

Aria cast Vic a veiled look. How much *had* he agreed to pay this woman?

She wasn't going to quibble though. Thanks to Greta and her ship, they were safe.

"I'm sorry we've given you so much trouble," she said, turning her attention back to the pilot. "But as you can probably tell, we were desperate."

Greta held her gaze for a moment before muttering another curse. She then swiveled back to face the instrument panel.

Aria sighed once more. She could unclip her harness now and move about the cabin. However, after what she'd been through, she was content just to sit. Likewise, Vic didn't rise from his seat.

Glancing his way once more, Aria found him watching her.

Her pulse quickened at the intensity of his gaze. She longed then to sink into his embrace, for his arms to go around her and hold her tight.

# 28. A COSTLY ERROR

AS SOON AS he heard the cargo ship's engines start, Elijah began kicking his way out. It was hard work with his ankles and wrists bound. However, he managed to brace himself against the back of the locker and slam the soles of his boots hard against the metal door.

Jaw clenched, he put his whole weight behind each kick, fury and frustration pulsing through him.

Curse that cyborg. Gods, he was strong. Elijah was no weakling, but it had been like fighting off a battle-droid earlier. His belly and ribs still ached, and his head hurt from the blow that had knocked him sideways outside the virology lab.

He'd heard their conversation earlier, had smelt the chemical odor of fast-acting epoxy resin as they'd applied it to the door.

His way out was jammed for the moment, but that door wouldn't withstand a hammering.

His arms were bound behind him, so he couldn't access his wrist-comm to call for help. But after what he'd helped Aria do earlier, it was best he didn't. Best he got out of here without any of his staff, or his brother, learning about what had happened to him.

It took a while to break it open, and when the metal gave way under the heel of his boot, sweat was streaming down Elijah's face.

He then wriggled his way out of the space, across the grease-stained floor, and onto the metal walkway that ringed the landing bay.

Rolling into a sitting position, Elijah's gaze swept the brightly lit space, traveling to the empty docking station where the *CS Vertigo* had been parked.

Yes, he'd taken note of the faded name on the ship's hull as they'd boarded earlier.

Elijah's already bruised gut clenched, bitterness filling his mouth.

He didn't understand Aria's behavior. In retrospect, he'd been a bit heavy-handed in his methods, but he'd been trying to do her a favor by not letting her leave Platinum 5. She knew now that he had a conscience, that he wasn't going to use the Starellusbacter against his enemies. He'd wanted to protect her, to ensure Lucas didn't find her, or blame her, when he went on the rampage.

He'd wondered initially why she'd fought him, but as soon as he'd seen his fiancée and Mir-Riorde interact, realization had dawned. The Destroyer take them both, they were lovers.

The realization had felt like a second punch to the stomach, an added humiliation. Why had Aria taken up with a cyborg? Elijah was a clan-lord; he could give her anything she wanted, but she didn't care.

He thought back to when they'd been children, hiding from his father's battle-droids on Alpha deck, and then later as teenagers when their friendship had deepened. They'd sit for hours on the rec-deck, sharing secrets. Growing up the eldest of three brothers, he'd become used to watching his back. Elijah, Lucas, and Tian had always been rivals, yet he'd been able to talk to Aria, trust her.

Elijah's mouth flattened into a thin line then as something tugged deep in his chest. The connection they'd once shared was gone now; Aria was lost to him.

A tall, cloaked figure appeared at the far end of the walkway, making its way toward one of the ships with a long, loping stride.

Struggling to his knees, Elijah gave a strangled cry.

Red-hot humiliation flooded over him; he hated feeling this helpless. He couldn't even raise a hand or call properly for help.

The stranger saw him then, their pace faltering.

Elijah made another choking noise, and the cloaked figure resumed walking, closing the gap between them. As they neared, he caught a glimpse of silvery-green skin, a brow ridge, and gills.

Reaching him, the Daksari bent low and ripped the tape off Elijah's mouth.

Stinging, burning pain scalded his lips, and Elijah choked out a curse. Shit, that had hurt. He then glanced up into a pair of curious golden eyes. "Free me," he rasped.

Elijah seethed throughout the entire journey back to Alpha. Striding along the moving walkway, hood pulled up once more, he went over the events of the past few hours, marking every detail. Anger was easier to deal with than hurt—Aria and her cyborg lover had made a fool of him, and his first instinct was revenge.

However, he quashed the urge. He needed to think straight right now.

There was no use alerting his space fleet about the *CS Vertigo* just yet. They wouldn't find the freighter easily anyway, for it would have already jumped into hyperspace and could be anywhere in the sector at present. His commanders would also have questions about the ship they were hunting, ones he had to be ready to answer.

No, he needed to sidestep his rage, his disappointment, and look to cover his own ass.

He'd just helped destroy Lucas's work. His brother would be apoplectic, would be searching for the culprit.

The blame could be laid on Aria and her accomplice, but Elijah would have to be careful.

He needed to form a plan. He also had to tie up some loose ends.

The Starellusbacter had been dealt with, but the scientists who'd developed it hadn't been. Doctor Varis and his associates were about to find their glowing careers unceremoniously ended.

An elevator whisked Elijah up to Alpha deck. As he stepped out into the wide colonnaded atrium, with a sweeping, transparent roof overhead, he glanced down at his wrist-comm.

It was the early hours of the morning—time for him to retire.

Massive bronze doors, embossed with the Mir-Ferrin crest, loomed before him. Towering battle-droids flanked the entrance, heavy laser-rifles held at the ready.

Elijah pushed back the hood of his cloak as he approached so they could get a good look at him.

He was grateful droids, not sentients, guarded Alpha. Battle-droids didn't ask questions. They wouldn't be suspicious that their clan-lord was out and about at this hour.

Entering Alpha, Elijah traveled the network of colonnaded walkways to his apartments. He passed another pair of battle-droids guarding the area before stepping into his sanctuary.

Inside the lounge—a calm space lined with over-stuffed dark-bronze sofas, and with soft furs over the polished white floors—he kicked off his boots, removed his cloak, and walked over to the sideboard.

His insides were still in knots, and he was tempted to pour himself something strong. However, his throat was dry, and he needed to keep his mind clear.

Pouring himself a glass of water, he drained it in a couple of gulps. He then poured himself another before padding barefoot over to the floor-to-ceiling windows, his gaze alighting on Formidian's topaz and cream surface.

"Damn you, Lucas," he muttered then, his fingers clenching around the glass. If it hadn't been for his brother's scheming, Aria would never have overheard them on their wedding day—she'd never have run.

Yet deep down, Elijah knew he too had to shoulder some of the blame. He'd let desperation overrule good sense over the past months, and although he'd realized his mistake and tried to put things right, it had been too late.

His error had cost him dearly.

His wrist-comm started bleeping urgently then, rousing him from his brooding.

A name flashed up on the screen. Jaw clenching, he accepted the call.

"Haris, what is it?" he demanded tersely.

"Apologies for the late hour, My Lord." The commander's gravelly voice echoed through the lounge. "But there's been an explosion."

Elijah's breathing stilled, and even before Haris Mir-Ferrin continued, he knew what was coming.

"The virology lab on Delta has been destroyed."

Aria tilted her head up, gasping. Warm water cascaded over her neck and chest, although she wasn't focused on that right now, but instead on the pulsing waves of pleasure that rippled out from her lower belly. Bracing herself against the walls of the cramped cubicle, she leaned back into Vic, giving herself up to the sensation of him buried deep inside her.

He'd just given her a delicious orgasm. In the aftermath, she hung there limp and trembling in his embrace.

Vic's arms wrapped around her torso then, his lips trailing up her neck to the shell of her ear. "Aria," he whispered huskily.

Her breathing caught at the raw emotion in his voice.

Lowering a hand from the wall, she placed it over his, squeezing firmly. "Vic," she murmured back, her own voice catching. Wis, her chest ached from the force of what she felt for this man.

This was their first private moment together since boarding the *CS Vertigo*—a shower in the ship's tiny bathroom. They were around five hours into the long journey to Cadex 12, and the adrenaline of their success and subsequent escape had started to fade.

Climbing into the cubicle together, they'd washed each other. But what started as a tender moment quickly turned steamy—and before Aria knew it, she was bracing herself against the slippery walls while Vic pounded into her from behind.

"I thought I'd lost you back there," he admitted then, his hold on her tightening. "When you activated the emergency signal, and I couldn't get inside the lab to save you … I felt helpless." His tone roughened further. "I hated not knowing what was happening."

Aria's throat tightened as she recalled his fury when he'd punched Elijah to the ground and stood over him, pistol raised.

He'd been close to blowing his head off, and would have, if she hadn't intervened.

"I was afraid as well," she admitted. "But I knew you were waiting outside." She wove her fingers through his, sinking her shoulders into the hard strength of his chest. "I knew I could rely on you."

Silence fell before his hold on her tightened. "I never thought I'd have this," he said softly. "I'd gotten used to being a loner after the transitioning … told myself I was happier that way … but you crashed into my life and showed me what I was missing. I'd take on the whole galaxy to protect you, Aria."

Warmth spread across Aria's chest at his admission, his declaration.

She had no doubt he would.


"That was a long shower," Greta announced when Aria and Vic emerged into the cabin. "I suppose you've used up all the hot water?"

"We have," Vic replied, his tone dry. "Sorry about that."

He didn't sound sorry at all, and Aria dug him in the ribs with her elbow before flashing Greta a contrite smile.

The captain's gaze glinted then, making it evident she knew exactly what her passengers had gotten up to in the bathroom. Stepping down from the cockpit, where Frol was hunched over the console, running diagnostics,

Greta crossed to the small food replicator in the corner of the cabin. "I'm going to eat … do you want anything?"

Aria's belly rumbled at the suggestion. She'd been too nervous to enjoy food since her last meal on the passenger liner, but she was light-headed with hunger now.

"Yes, thanks," she replied.

"Take a seat then."

Aria and Vic slid into the low bench seat at the table, looking on as Greta punched at the digital display on the replicator.

"Choices are limited," she admitted, casting them a veiled glance. "It's a root-vegetable stew, omelet, or fried fish."

"I'll have the omelet," Aria answered.

"Same here," Vic added.

"Okay … three omelets," Greta instructed the machine. The replicator started to whirr, and a short while later, she carried three steaming plates across to the table.

Aria took a bite of hers and winced. "Gods … it's like rubber."

Greta shrugged and took a large forkful of hers. "Trust me, it's one of the better dishes."

Swallowing her mouthful of rubbery egg, Aria dug her fork into the unappetizing omelet. Likewise, Vic ate with grim determination.

"Where are you from, Greta?" Aria asked after a brief pause.

"Caldoros … my family serves the Mir-Lelith clan-lord."

"But you don't?" Vic was watching Greta now, his gaze steady.

She pulled a face. "No."

"Too boring for you?"

"Something like that."

Aria observed Greta with interest. The captain of the *CS Vertigo* was still reasonably young, but there was a jaded edge to her that belied her round, youthful face.

Noting her look, Greta frowned before digging her fork into her omelet once more. "No questions … remember? It works both ways."

# 29. FAMILY

ELIJAH WAS IN a meeting with his commanders when Lucas barged into the conference room.

Looking up from the report he was discussing, Elijah's gaze alighted on his younger brother's belligerent red face. Gone was Lucas's smarmy smile, and what replaced it wasn't pretty. "Doctor Varis and his assistants have gone missing," Lucas announced, his sharp voice carrying across the room. "I want answers."

Their gazes fused and held for a few moments before Elijah sighed. He'd been waiting for Lucas to confront him, although his brother had poor timing.

"Can't this wait?"

His brother's jaw bunched. "No."

Elijah leaned back in his seat, his gaze sweeping the stern faces of his commanders seated around him. They'd been discussing the destruction of the virology lab, and the various hypotheses for who was responsible. Of course, none who served him knew of the part their clan-lord had played in the events of the night before.

"We shall continue this discussion later," he addressed his commanders. "Leave us."

Rising from their seats, they obeyed him.

Elijah waited until the last bronze-and-black-clad figure had departed the conference room, the doors sliding closed behind them, before he spoke. "Sit down, Lucas."

His brother ignored him. Instead, he approached the table and leaned forward, placing his palms upon its polished surface. "Are you behind this?"

Elijah quirked an eyebrow. "Excuse me?"

"First someone destroys the laboratory, and then my lead scientist and his assistants disappear from their quarters." Lucas's gaze bored into him. "Neither of these happenings is a coincidence … and only someone with high-level clearance has such authorization."

Elijah snorted. "You think I'd damage my own space station?" he drawled. "Or rid myself of valuable staff?"

Lucas's dark brows crashed together. Elijah spied the doubt on his face, the confusion. Lucas was sharp-witted, but he was having trouble making sense of what had just happened.

Of course, Elijah *was* behind the disappearance of the scientists.

The moment he'd cut his call with Commander Haris hours earlier, he'd issued an order to his personal squad of battle-droids.

They'd trooped down to Delta, moving easily amongst the chaos that reigned on the deck, before yanking Doctor Varis and his assistants from their beds. Within the hour, the scientists were on board a transport ship bound for a prison colony.

Once again, battle-droids followed his orders without question.

If Lucas started digging into the droids' memory logs, he'd likely discover the truth—but Elijah would ensure they were erased by the end of the day.

"Have the security cameras turned up anything?" he asked after a lengthy pause. It surprised him how calm he was, how easy it was to lie to his brother.

But despite that his stomach clenched every time his thoughts strayed to Aria, he never lost sight of why he'd gone down to the virology lab in the dead of night in the first place.

Things had gone far enough.

They'd lock horns again with the Mir-Brennans soon enough, but it would be a clean fight.

Lucas had to be leashed.

His brother's face screwed up. Pushing back from the table, he folded his arms across his chest. "We have footage of a female Nandoon entering the lab an hour after it closed for the evening."

"A Nandoon?"

Lucas's gaze glinted. "We don't have her identity … someone wiped the security log on the door … around the same time as they disabled the cameras." His features tightened. "All files relating to the bacterium are gone now too. All the research notes deleted."

Elijah inclined his head, schooling his features into a scowl.

His brother continued to stare at him. "I repeat … you need high-level clearance to be able to do any of that."

"Then we need to do a sweep of everyone who has it. If we have a traitor in our midst, I want them found." Elijah paused then, leaning forward. "Perhaps Doctor Varis and his team are behind this … it seems a coincidence they'd disappear on the night the virology lab is destroyed."

A nerve ticked in Lucas's cheek, discomfort rippling over his face. "Doctor Varis wouldn't betray me."

Elijah viewed him, careful to keep his expression dispassionate, even as his pulse quickened. He had Lucas where he wanted him now. "Really, brother? Would you stake your life on it?"

"You're giving her your ship?"

Vic nodded, tearing his gaze from where Aria stared at him, her lips parted in shock, and glancing over at where Greta stood a few feet away silently admiring the lines of her new freighter.

She was looking pleased with the deal she'd made, and Vic didn't blame her.

The *CS Vertigo* was docked next to *The Wayfarer* in this private landing bay on Cadex 12—and seeing the two ships next to each other made the contrast between them evident.

The Mir-Lelith cargo ship was shabby, rusted, and falling to pieces, while his freighter was streamlined Lazda steel.

Vic's gut twisted then.

He couldn't believe he was giving *The Wayfarer* up, but he was.

Frol gave an excited yip and scurried over to the freighter, running furry hands over its fuselage. The sight of the Gibbit caressing his ship made the knots in Vic's stomach tighten further.

Pushing aside the urge to grab Frol by the scruff and haul him away from *The Wayfarer*, Vic approached the hatch. He punched in the security code and a moment later, it lowered with a hiss of hydraulics.

"Obsidian," he called. "Get out here."

The thump of heavy, rubber-soled feet followed, and the tall black droid appeared in the doorway.

Obsidian's gaze flicked to where Frol was making crooning sounds as he examined the freighter's shields, before the droid focused on the statuesque woman standing a few feet away. "Aria," Obsidian rasped. "You have returned."

"I have," Aria replied, her mouth curving, even if her green eyes were troubled. "It's good to see you again, Obsidian."

"Does the droid come with the ship?" Greta asked.

Vic shook his head. "Obsidian has a mind of his own. He decides whom he works with." He glanced back at his first mate. "I'm handing over *The Wayfarer* to a new owner ... go get the ship's papers."

Obsidian didn't move—and although its gaze wasn't sentient, Vic could almost see the accusation there. "A new owner?" the droid queried.

"Yes ... we needed passage off Platinum 5, and it was expensive."

"You never told me you used your freighter to pay for it?" Aria spoke up then. Her face had gone taut as she met his eye once more.

"Would it have mattered?"

She swallowed. They both knew the truth of it. They'd been desperate and limited in choices and resources, especially after her PCSD was stolen.

Inhaling sharply, Vic turned back to Greta. The woman was watching him with a shrewd look. She knew exactly what he was giving up, and what it was costing him. Her gaze narrowed then. "The freighter isn't stolen, is it?"

"She's legal … all the same, I'd give her a new name and registration before departing Cadex 12 if I were you."

Greta nodded, mouth thinning. "Good idea."

Vic shifted his attention from the pilot, his gaze traveling over the sleek lines of his freighter. *The Wayfarer* had been his home, a part of him, for the past six years—but his life, and his priorities, had changed.

As much as it cut him up to do so, it was time to give her up.

Aria terminated her call to Lady Jenna and turned to where Vic and Obsidian waited.

She then flashed them a smile. "It's done … a private shuttle will be on its way shortly from Staturine II to collect us."

Vic's mouth twitched. "Good."

He moved close then to the window where Aria had been viewing the passenger liners departing and arriving from the landing bays below. Observing his profile, Aria wondered how he was feeling about leaving *The Wayfarer* behind.

Obsidian had accepted the news with stoicism, although the droid now seemed a bit lost as it stood on the viewing deck, two duffel bags containing Vic's meager possessions at its feet.

"What now?" she murmured.

He glanced her way. "It looks like we're going back to Staturine II."

Nervousness fluttered in her belly. She knew he wanted to be with her, but she didn't like how much he was prepared to sacrifice to do so. Although it wasn't always an easy life, Vic had enjoyed traveling the sector with Obsidian onboard *The Wayfarer*. "Lady Jenna has offered me a place in her household ... and a position at a research institute in Briscay." Aria paused then. "Are you happy to live in Castle Valnor with me?"

His hazel eye gleamed. "I was also offered a position there, remember? Captain of the Lady's Watch."

"And you'll take it?"

He held her gaze, the moment drawing out. "I used to be against the idea ... I couldn't stand the thought of being bound to anyone, or anything, again. But that was before I met you."

Her mouth quirked. "And you don't mind working for Lady Jenna?"

He snorted. "No."

She raised her eyebrows. "Really?"

"I'll admit I was a bit bitter about how she used you to her own ends ... but now everything has ended well, I'll try to let it go."

Aria smiled. "I imagine it's an honor to be offered such a position."

"It is."

Warmth spread across her chest. At least they'd be able to make a fresh start together on Staturine II. Elijah would likely be after them now, out for revenge, but in Castle Valnor, they'd be under Mir-Brennan protection. Even the Mir-Ferrin clan-lord's long reach couldn't stretch there.

Aria wasn't a Mir-Brennan, and her clan was a Mir-Ferrin ally, but her father had betrayed her trust, while her ex-fiancé treated her like his property. She'd turned her back on them both now.

"And what about Obsidian?" she murmured, glancing over at the battle-droid once more. It was watching them steadily.

Vic turned to face the droid. "You're free. You know that, don't you?"

Obsidian nodded. "I've traveled with you out of choice, Vic," it replied, its raspy voice oddly subdued, "but I've no role now. Even if I accompany you to Staturine II, what will I do there?"

"You'll join the Watch," Vic said without hesitation. "You'll be my lieutenant."

Obsidian cocked its head. "The clan-lady will permit it?"

Vic stepped closer and placed a hand on the droid's shoulder. "I will ensure she does."

Watching them, Aria's throat constricted. The galaxy was full of waifs and strays. Some individuals, like her, were estranged from, or rejected by, their families. Others, like Vic, had lost theirs. But there were a few, like Obsidian, who never had a family, or a clan, to begin with. The battle-droid had been reprogrammed after Vic took it from Platinum 5, but somewhere along the way in the past years, it had developed a very unmechanical bond to the cyborg it worked alongside.

Vic was the closest thing Obsidian had to kin.

"We're not leaving you behind, Obsidian." She moved close then, taking hold of the droid's metal hand and squeezing tightly. "We're family ... and we need to stick together."

The battle-droid's gaze swiveled to her. "Family?"

Aria smiled. "That's right."

She reached out then with her free hand and slipped it into Vic's grip before shifting her attention from the droid to her lover.

The seconds drew out.

Vic's gaze gleamed. "That's right."

# 30. HEROES

"HERE'S TO ARIA and Vic … both heroes. I just hope you realize how much I appreciate your bravery."

The Mir-Brennan clan-lady raised a flute of sparkling wine aloft, while around her, those seated at the long table did the same. Malik, Isla, and Beatrix were all present for this celebratory dinner.

Studying Lady Jenna's face, Aria noted how the woman's eyes shone with emotion. Next to her, Malik's mouth curved, while Bea was grinning. Even Isla, who usually looked so somber, wore an enigmatic smile.

"We *all* appreciate what you did," Malik added. He then shifted his attention to where Vic sat at Aria's side. His mouth quirked. "I knew you'd go after her."

Vic snorted, yet he didn't deny it.

Aria's lips lifted at the corners. "We make a good team," she murmured.

The overhead pendant lights sparkled off the rims of their flutes as they held them aloft in a toast.

Aria took a sip of the dry, sparkling wine, and sighed as the bubbles bit at the back of her throat. It felt good to celebrate their success, to focus on what they'd done.

Because of her and Vic, the Mir-Ferrins no longer had a bioweapon to wield against their enemies.

Jenna shook her head as she lowered her glass, a rueful expression upon her face now. "I still can't believe Elijah Mir-Ferrin came down to the lab to destroy the bacteria while you were there."

"You can imagine my shock when I turned around to find him standing behind me," Aria replied. That was an understatement—her heart had nearly stopped. "It's an irony the clan-lord was complicit in what we did." She cocked an eyebrow then. "However, I bet he got a shock when the virology lab blew up … just as well I set the charge before he turned up."

"I'm surprised you didn't kill him while you had the chance," Isla spoke up then. Aria shifted her attention to where the slim, dark-haired woman looked on. As usual, her sea-blue eyes were veiled, and the half-smile Aria had glimpsed just moments before had gone. "You'd have done us all a favor."

"My finger was twitching on the trigger," Vic admitted. "But Aria convinced me not to … and in the end, she was right." He paused then. "The Starellusbacter was his brother's project. I even considered abducting Elijah and handing him over to Lady Jenna as a political hostage … but I decided against it. You really don't want Lucas Mir-Ferrin in charge."

Silence followed these words, and all their expressions sobered.

The Mir-Brennans and the Mir-Ferrins were enemies still, and when Lady Jenna launched her assault to regain Idral, they'd be in open conflict once more. But at least there wasn't a biological weapon in the mix now.

Personally, Aria was relieved Vic had listened to her and not killed Elijah. He was highly protective of her, something she appreciated, but ending the clan-lord's life wouldn't change anything. And despite everything, she couldn't forget that she and Elijah had once been friends; she'd once wanted to be his wife. He was a ruthless leader, as his father and grandfather had been before him, but he was neither a madman nor a tyrant.

Not yet, anyway.

"Malik tells me you have reconsidered my offer, Vic," Lady Jenna said after a lengthy pause. The clan-lady was watching Vic, a speculative glint in her eye. "Will you captain the Lady's Watch, after all?"

Vic's gaze met hers across the table. "If the offer still stands, My Lady?"

Jenna's lips curved. "It does." She held Vic's gaze a moment longer before her smile faltered. "You think me merciless, don't you?"

"It came as a shock to see you push Aria into such a dangerous mission," Vic admitted with his usual bluntness.

The clan-lady sighed, leaning back in her seat and clasping her fingers around the stem of her glass that sat on the table in front of her. "I used to watch my father and brother rule, and wonder how they managed it," she murmured. "Cathal was always so calm, so clear-headed about what was necessary." She paused then, her gaze flicking to Aria. "I saw an opportunity, and I took it … but I don't think you're expendable. I'm sorry if I gave either of you that impression."

"It doesn't matter now," Aria assured her. And it didn't—not to her. They'd come out the other side unscathed. "Sometimes risks have to be taken for the greater good." Reaching out under the table, she placed a hand on Vic's knee and gently squeezed. "It's like your clan motto says … 'glory is the reward of valor'."

Vic sighed and leaned back against the side of the deep tub. His eye then fluttered shut. "I could get used to this."

"So could I," Aria murmured. "I think I could live in this spa bath."

Vic huffed a laugh before opening his eye.

Aria sat opposite him, up to her neck in suds that smelled like tropical flowers. Her thick chestnut hair was piled up on the crown of her head, revealing her long neck, and her coppery skin glistened.

She was smiling at him, and warmth that had nothing to do with the hot water he was soaking in spread out from under his breastbone. Gods, she was a sight.

He could certainly get used to relaxing in this tub with Aria, to listening to the musical lilt of her voice as the heat of the water drew the tension out of his muscles.

Vic shifted his attention to the wide floor-to-ceiling window before them. From up here, they looked east, over Briscay's botanic gardens. Beneath them spread a carpet of different hues of green—lime, emerald, and jade—nestled amongst the skeletal outlines of deciduous trees. They were in the midst of Staturine II's long winter; outdoors the air was cold and damp. Beyond the gardens, a high spine of mountains, glistening white in the afternoon sun, sliced across a pale blue sky.

And as Vic gazed upon the view, he spied a shuttle swoop overhead—golden with the Mir-Brennan insignia emblazoned on the side. The clan-lady had called her commanders to her for a meeting to let them know what had transpired and to discuss the way forward. Vic guessed that was one of them arriving now, for *The Star Tempest* was currently orbiting Staturine II.

"Sparkling water?"

Vic glanced away from the view to where a silver and gold utility-droid floated into the bathroom, one clawed hand holding a tray with frosted glasses aloft.

"Thanks, EDY50," he replied, reaching out and taking a glass. Aria did likewise.

EDY50 was a gift from Lady Jenna, as was this luxurious apartment. They'd been here a day, and Vic still couldn't believe this was his life now. He wasn't used to living surrounded by so much space and comfort.

"Will there be anything else?" the droid chirped.

"No, that's it for the moment," Aria replied, flashing EDY50 a smile.

The utility-droid floated out of the bathroom, leaving them alone once more.

"It does feel strange, doesn't it?" Aria said, taking a sip of water. "To live like this."

Vic's mouth twitched. "You're the daughter of a clan-lord ... surely, this isn't too difficult for you?"

Aria snorted. "The Mir-Strakens don't live like the Mir-Brennans, let me assure you. My clan prefers practicality to opulence."

Vic glimpsed the shadow that flitted across her face at the mention of her clan. No doubt, it reminded Aria of her father. After Morgan Mir-Straken had confirmed he was responsible for having a bug implanted in her back, Aria had broken with him.

Her father had given her little choice, yet Vic could see his betrayal saddened her; it likely would for some time to come.

"When do you start work?" he asked, hoping to draw her attention from her father and chase those shadows away. Vic liked to see Aria happy.

"Lady Jenna's going to escort me to the laboratory tomorrow," she replied, her mouth lifting into a half-smile. "I'm going to be leading my own team of researchers."

Vic drained his glass of water and set it aside on the rim of the bath. "And are you looking forward to it?"

She sighed. "I think so. A month ago, if I'd been offered such a position, I'd have been overjoyed, but now there's a part of me that wishes we were still onboard *The Wayfarer* … just you, me, and Obsidian, traveling the sector together." She paused then, her emerald gaze spearing his. "We did the right thing, didn't we … coming to live here?"

Vic reached forward and took her by the hand, drawing her across the tub and onto his lap. He then removed her glass and set it down next to his. "Second thoughts?"

Aria stared down into his face. "I don't know," she murmured. "You?"

Lifting his hand, he stroked her cheek, leaving a trail of bubbles upon her skin. "No. Sometimes a chapter of your life ends, and it's time to begin another," he replied. "This new start is right for us. It'll just take some getting used to, that's all."

Aria nodded. Her lips curved then. "I forgot to ask how your first day with the Watch went."

"Well enough … they're all wary of me though. They've never taken orders from a cyborg before."

"So, how does it feel … to have your team call you 'Captain'?"

"Strange … although I get the feeling Obsidian loves being addressed as 'Lieutenant'."

Aria laughed, and the warm sound echoed through the bathroom. "I bet he does."

Vic stroked her cheek once more and then skimmed the pad of his thumb across her full lower lip. "It'll all work out, Aria," he said softly. "No matter what the future holds, what's important is that we're together."

# EPILOGUE: WELL PLAYED

**Six months later …**

"KEEP CIRCLING ME, Aria. It's much harder to grab a moving target."

"I am moving—oomph."

Aria flew backward as Vic tackled her, and they landed together on the padded floor of the combat ring.

Muttering a curse, Aria rolled out from under him and scrambled to her feet. "Let's go again."

Vic got up with a sigh and turned to her. "All right. Once more then."

Pale afternoon sunlight filtered across the courtyard—one of the many that dotted Castle Valnor's vast dove-grey keep. Now that the interminable winter had ended and spring had finally started, the sun had a little warmth to it and the evenings were drawing out.

Aria had finished work for the day and taken a shunt home through Briscay's bustling streets. Twice a week, before dinner, Vic had agreed to teach her some hand-to-hand combat skills. However, although Vic assured Aria she was making good progress, she was growing frustrated at how easily he still bested her.

True, he was a cyborg, and stronger and faster than most men. Nonetheless, she'd have liked to get the upper hand, just once, in a fight.

They started to circle each other once more, and Aria was grateful they were alone in the courtyard. She didn't want an audience while Vic landed her on her back, time after time. All the same, she enjoyed these sessions. The physical exertion, after a day bent over a microscope and managing a lab, was a welcome release, and she liked being close to Vic.

The black sleeveless vest and close-fitting leggings he wore molded to his strong, muscular frame, and a light sheen covered his bare arms and face—like her, he was beginning to sweat.

"You need to start anticipating me better," Vic instructed while they continued to circle each other. He made a grab for her, and she deflected it with her forearm before jumping out of reach. "Don't just react … think ahead." He paused then, his mouth twitching. "You've fought me enough times now to know my fighting style. Think … is there anything you can use to your advantage."

Aria's brow furrowed. Vic was quick and lethal. She especially enjoyed watching him spar with Malik, for Jenna's consort was easily his equal when it came to physical combat. She thought then to the times she'd seen Malik when their bouts had ended in his favor, and the tricks he'd employed.

She recalled that Malik always followed up a defensive move with a swift, vicious attack. He never gave his opponent a chance to anticipate him.

Jaw firming, she readied herself, and when Vic lunged for her once more, she deflected his arm again, but instead of jumping out of range, as she usually did, she ducked under his guard, kicked him in the shins, and then drove her elbow into his solar plexus.

Vic's grunt of surprise followed. However, he rallied fast, grabbing her in a headlock as her elbow went for his stomach.

Aria dropped down and braced a hand against his thigh. An instant later, her hand moved from there to his groin.

Vic froze. "That's a dirty move," he growled.

Smiling, Aria gave the bulge she cupped a light squeeze. "A man's most vulnerable spot … and you left it unprotected."

He snorted, releasing her. "Well played."

Grinning now, Aria straightened up and pushed a lock of hair that had escaped from her braid out of her eyes. "Well … I learned from the best."

Breathing hard, they faced each other.

"You've improved a lot over the last few sessions, you know?" Vic said after a moment. "I should let you spar with one of my team sometime."

"I enjoy it," she admitted, still smiling. "Thank you for teaching me." Moving close to him, she leaned in and brushed her lips over his.

In response, he pulled her close and kissed her.

Momentarily forgetting where they were, Aria linked her arms around his neck, molding herself against him. When they finally broke apart, she didn't let him go. Instead, her hands encircled his back as she buried her face in the crook of his neck, breathing in the spicy, musky scent of his skin.

"I realized something today," she murmured then.

"What's that?"

"I'm bored at work."

Soft laughter rumbled across his chest. "What?"

She drew back, her gaze snaring his. "This is no laughing matter … science used to be my life." She paused then, her chest tightening. In truth, she'd been wanting to broach this subject with Vic for days now. For the first few weeks here in Briscay, everything had been new and exciting—but with the passing of the months, she'd begun to realize something about herself.

Meeting Vic and traveling with him and Obsidian had changed her.

He'd stirred up a latent restlessness, and these days, whenever she was at the lab, she found herself daydreaming about working alongside Vic. That was why she'd asked him to teach her to fight. Working as a trader, and sometimes smuggler, could be risky, and she wanted to be able to defend herself.

Wishing she could read his face, Aria cleared her throat and released her hold on him. "Please, tell me you hate being Captain of the Lady's Watch ... that you want to go back to your old job."

His hazel eye glinted. "I don't *hate* my role here." Her stomach clenched at these words, yet he continued. "But I do miss the freedom of my old life ... and so does Obsidian. We were talking about it yesterday."

"You were?"

He nodded. "I told him that your career was important to you ... and that we'd have to stay." He took hold of her hands then, squeezing gently. "So, it isn't anymore?"

Aria shook her head. "I feel as if I'm being slowly suffocated." She pulled a face. "Of course, we don't have a ship now ... and they're expensive."

"Don't worry about that," he replied. "Jenna compensated me for *The Wayfarer*. Credits aren't an issue."

Her pulse quickened at this news. "When shall we hand in our notices then?"

His gaze held hers. "The Mir-Brennans are gearing up to take back Idral ... the strike will come in the next six months. As soon as it's done, you, me, and Obsidian, can go our own way. Are you able to wait that long?"

Aria nodded. She understood why he wanted to remain at the clan-lady's side until the Mir-Brennans had taken back Idral. Vic was loyal; it was one of the many things she adored about him. She could do another six months if she knew they had plans to leave.

"I love you," she murmured.

He lifted her hand to his lips and kissed the back of it.

And when he glanced up at her, to her surprise and delight, his mouth curved into a half-smile.

**The End**

# ABOUT THE AUTHOR

Samantha Charlton is a multi-award-winning author of Amazon best-selling Historical Romances, writing under a nom de plume. However, she doesn't just have a passion for the past, but also the future. She fell in love with Han Solo at an early age and began a lifelong love of Sci-Fi adventure and Space Opera. This led her to write Space Opera—with emotional and steamy romance—of her own!

**Connect with Sam online:**
www.samanthacharltonauthor.com
www.facebook.com/samanthacharltonauthor
Email: samanthajcharlton@gmail.com